P9-EGL-608

Michael Moorcock

THE MAD GOD'S AMULET

Volume Two of the History of the Runestaff

DAW BOOKS, INC.
DONALD A. WOLLHEIM, PUBLISHER

1301 Avenue of the Americas
New York, N. Y.   10019

For Jim Cawthorn,
for his inspiration and his drawings.

FIRST DAW PRINTING, APRIL 1977

1 2 3 4 5 6 7 8 9

PRINTED IN U.S.A.

Contents

BOOK ONE

WE HAVE LEARNED now how Dorian Hawkmoon, last Duke of Köln, one aspect of the Champion Eternal, threw off the power of the Black Jewel and saved the city of Hamadan from conquest by the Dark Empire of Granbretan. His arch-enemy, Baron Meliadus, defeated, Hawkmoon set off westward again, bound for the besieged Kamarg, where his betrothed, Yisselda, Count Brass's daughter, awaited him. With his boon companion Oladahn, beast-man of the Bulgar Mountains, Hawkmoon rode from Persia toward the Cyprian Sea and the port of Tarabulus, where they hoped to find a ship brave enough to bear them back to the Kamarg. But in the Syranian Desert they lost their way and came close to dying of thirst and exhaustion before they saw the peaceful ruins of Soryandum lying at the foot of a range of green hills on which wild sheep grazed. . . .

Meanwhile, in Europe, the Dark Empire extended its terrible rule, while elsewhere the Runestaff pulsed, exerting its influence over thousands of miles to involve the destinies of some several human souls of disparate character and ambitions. . . .

—*The High History of the Runestaff*

sands of stone, stood plenty of trad
the innkeeper, even in this remote town,
of him and let them in.

That night they sat in the public room of the
sweet wine and talking to the members of

Chapter One

SORYANDUM

THE CITY WAS old, begrimed by time. A place of
wind-worn stones and tumbled masonry, its towers tilt-
ing and its walls crumbling. Wild sheep cropped the
grass that grew between cracked paving stones, bright-
plumed birds nested among columns of faded mosaic.
The city had once been splendid and terrible; now it was
beautiful and tranquil. The two travellers came to it in
the mellow haze of the morning, when a melancholy
wind blew through the silence of the ancient streets.
The hooves of the horses were hushed as the travellers
led them between towers that were green with age,
passed by ruins bright with blossoms of orange, ochre
and purple. And this was Soryandum, deserted by its
folk.

The men and their horses were turned all one colour
by the dust that caked them, making them resemble
statues that had come to life. They moved slowly, looking wonderingly about them at the beauty of the dead
city.

The first man was tall and lean, and although weary
he moved with the graceful stride of the trained warrior. His long fair hair had been bleached near white
by the sun, and his pale blue eyes had a hint of madness in the. But the thing most remarkable about his
appearance was the dull black jewel sunk into his forehead just above and between the eyes, a stigmata he

owed to the perverted miracle workings of the sorcerer-scientists of Granbretan. His name was Dorian Hawkmoon, Duke von Köln, driven from his hereditary lands by the conquests of the Dark Empire, which schemed to rule the world. Dorian Hawkmoon, who had sworn vengeance against the most powerful nation on his war-tormented planet.

The creature who followed Hawkmoon bore a large bone bow and a quiver of arrows on his back. He was clad only in a pair of britches and boots of soft, floppy leather, but the whole of his body, including his face, was covered in red, wiry hair. His head came to just below Hawkmoon's shoulder. This was Oladahn, cross-bred offspring of a sorcerer and a mountain giantess from the Bulgar Mountains.

Oladahn patted sand from his fur and looked perplexed. "Never have I seen a city so fair. Why is it deserted? Who could leave such a place?"

Hawkmoon, as was his habit when puzzled, rubbed at the dull black jewel in his forehead. "Perhaps disease—who knows? Let's hope that if it was disease, none of it lingers on. I'll speculate later, but not now. I'm sure I hear water somewhere—and that's my first requirement. Food's my second, sleep's my third—and thought, friend Oladahn, a very distant fourth. . . ."

In one of the city's plazas they found a wall of blue-gray rock that had been carved with flowing figures. From the eyes of one stone maiden fell pure spring water that splashed into a hollow fashioned below. Hawkmoon stooped and drank, wiping wet hands over his dusty face. He stepped back for Oladahn to drink, then led the horses forward to slake their thirst.

Hawkmoon reached into one of his saddlebags and took out the cracked and crumpled map that had been given him in Hamadan. His finger crept across the map until it came to rest on the word "Soryandum." He smiled with relief. "We are not too far off our original route," he said. "Beyond these hills the Euphrates flows and Tarabulus lies beyond it by about a week's journey.

We'll rest here for today and tonight, then continue on our way. Refreshed, we will travel more rapidly."

Oladahn grinned. "Aye, and you'd explore the city before we leave, I fancy." He splashed water on his fur, then bent to pick up his bow and quiver. "Now to attend to your second requirement—food. I'll not be gone long. I saw a wild ram in the hills. Tonight we'll dine off roast mutton." He remounted his horse and was away, riding for the broken gates of the city while Hawkmoon stripped off his clothes and plunged his hands into the cool spring water, gasping with a sense of utter luxury as he poured the water over his head and body. Then he took fresh clothing from the saddlebag, pulling on a silk shirt given him by Queen Frawbra of Hamadan and a pair of blue cotton britches with flaring bottoms. Glad to be out of the heavier leather and iron he had worn for protection's sake while crossing the desert in case any of the Dark Empire's men were following them, Hawkmoon donned a pair of sandals to complete his outfit. His only concession to his earlier fears was the sword he buckled about him.

It was scarcely possible that he could have been followed here, and besides, the city was so peaceful that he could not believe any kind of danger threatened.

Hawkmoon went to his horse and unsaddled it, then crossed to the shade of a ruined tower to lie with his back against it and await Oladahn and the mutton.

Noon came and went, and Hawkmoon began to wonder what had become of his friend. He dozed for another hour before real trepidation began to stir in him and he rose to resaddle his horse.

It was highly unlikely, Hawkmoon knew, that an archer as skilled as Oladahn would take so long in pursuit of one wild sheep. Yet there seemed to be no possible danger here. Perhaps Oladahn had grown weary and decided to sleep for an hour or two before hauling the carcass back. Even if that were all that was delaying him, Hawkmoon decided, he might need assistance.

He mounted his horse and rode through the streets

to the crumbling outer wall of the city and to the hills beyond. The horse seemed to recover much of its former energy as its hooves touched grass, and Hawkmoon had to shorten the rein, riding into the hills at a light canter.

Ahead was a herd of wild sheep led by a large, wise looking ram, perhaps the one Oladahn had mentioned, but there was no sign at all of the little beast-man.

"Oladahn!" Hawkmoon yelled, peering about him. "Oladahn!" But only muffled echoes answered him.

Hawkmoon frowned, then urged his horse into a gallop, riding up a hill taller than the rest in the hope that from this vantage point he would be able to see his friend. Wild sheep scattered before him as the horse raced over the springy grass. He reached the top of the hill and shielded his eyes from the glare of the sun. He stared in every direction, but there was no sign of Oladahn.

For some moments he continued to look around him, hoping to see some trace of his friend; then, as he gazed toward the city, he saw a movement near the plaza of the spring. Had his eyes tricked him, or had he seen a man entering the shadows of the streets that led off the eastern side of the plaza? Could Oladahn have returned by another route? If so, why hadn't he answered Hawkmoon's call?

Hawkmoon had a nagging sense of terror in the back of his mind now, but he still could not believe that the city itself offered any menace.

He spurred his horse back down the hillside and leaped it over a section of ruined wall.

Muffled by the dust, the horse's hooves thudded through the streets as Hawkmoon headed toward the plaza, crying Oladahn's name. But again he was answered only by echoes. In the plaza there was no sign of the little mountain man.

Hawkmoon frowned, almost certain now that he and Oladahn had not, after all, been alone in the city. Yet there was no sign of inhabitants.

He turned his horse toward the streets. As he did so his ears caught a faint sound from above. He looked upward, his eyes searching the sky, certain that he recognized the sound. At last he saw it—a distant black shape in the air overhead. Then sunlight flashed on metal, and the sound became distinct, a clanking and whirring of giant bronze wings. Hawkmoon's heart sank.

The thing descending from the sky was unmistakably an ornate ornithopter, wrought in the shape of a gigantic condor, enameled in blue, scarlet, and green. No other nation on Earth possessed such vessels. It was a flying machine of the Dark Empire of Granbretan.

Now Oladahn's disappearance was fully explained. The warriors of the Dark Empire were present in Soryandum. It was more than likely, too, that they had recognized Oladahn and knew that Hawkmoon could not be far away. And Hawkmoon was the Dark Empire's most hated opponent.

Chapter Two

HUILLAM d'AVERC

HAWKMOON MADE FOR the shadows of the street, hoping that he had not been seen by the ornithopter.

Could the Granbretanians have followed him all the way across the desert? It was unlikely. Yet what else explained their presence in this remote place?

Hawkmoon drew his great battle blade from its scabbard and then dismounted. In his clothes of thin silk and cotton he felt more than ordinarily vulnerable as he ran through the streets seeking cover.

Now the ornithopter flew only a few feet above the tallest towers of Soryandum, almost certainly searching for Hawkmoon, the man whom the King-Emperor Huon had sworn must be revenged upon for his "betrayal" of the Dark Empire. Hawkmoon might have slain Baron Meliadus at the battle of Hamadan, but without doubt King Huon had swiftly dispatched a new emissary upon the task of hunting down the hated Hawkmoon.

The young Duke of Köln had not expected to journey without danger, but he had not believed that he would be found so soon.

He came to a dark building, half in ruins, whose cool doorway offered shelter. He entered the building and found himself in a hallway with walls of pale, carved stone partly overgrown with soft mosses and blooming lichens. A stairway ran up one side of the hall, and Hawkmoon, blade in hand, climbed the winding, moss-carpeted steps for several flights until he found himself in a small room into which sunlight streamed through a gap in the wall where the stones had fallen away. Flattening himself against the wall and peering around the broken section, Hawkmoon saw a large part of the city, saw the ornithopter wheeling and dipping as its vulture-masked pilot searched the streets.

There was a tower of faded green granite not too distant. It stood roughly in the center of Soryandum, dominating the city. The ornithopter circled this for some time, and at first Hawkmoon guessed that the pilot believed him to be hidden there, but then the flying machine settled on the flat, battlement-surrounded roof of the tower. From somewhere below other figures emerged to join the pilot.

These men were evidently of Granbretan also. They were all clad in heavy armor and cloaks, with huge metal masks covering their heads, in spite of the heat. Such was the twisted nature of Dark Empire men that they could not rid themselves of their masks whatever the circumstances. They seemed to have a deeprooted psychological reliance on them.

The masks were of rust red and murky yellow, fashioned to resemble rampant wild boars, with fierce, jeweled eyes that blazed in the sunlight and great ivory tusks curling from the flaring snouts.

These, then, were men of the Order of the Boar, infamous in Europe for its savagery. There were six of them standing by their leader, a tall, slender man whose mask was of gold and bronze and much more delicately wrought—almost to the point of caricaturing the mask of the Order. The man leaned on the arms of two of his companions—one squat and bulky, the other virtually a giant, with naked arms and legs of almost inhuman hairiness. Was the leader ill or wounded? wondered Hawkmoon. There seemed to be something theatrical about the way he leaned on his men. Hawkmoon thought then that he knew who the Boar leader was. It was almost certainly the renegade Frenchman Huillam d'Averc, once a brilliant painter and architect, who had joined the cause of Granbretan long before they had conquered France. An enigma, D'Averc, but a dangerous man for all that he affected illness.

Now the Boar leader spoke to the vulture-masked pilot, who shook his head. Evidently he had not seen Hawkmoon, but he pointed toward the spot where Hawkmoon had abandoned his horse. D'Averc—if it was D'Averc—languidly signed to one of his men, who disappeared below, to re-emerge almost at once with a struggling, snarling Oladahn.

Relieved, Hawkmoon watched as two of the boar-masked warriors dragged Oladahn close to the battlements. At least his friend was alive.

Then the Boar leader signed again, and the vulture pilot leaned into the cockpit of his flying machine and withdrew a bell-shaped megaphone, which he handed to the giant on whose arm the leader still rested. The giant placed this close to the snout of his master's mask.

Suddenly the quiet air of the city was filled with the bored, world-weary voice of the Boar leader.

"Duke von Köln, we know that you are present in this city, for we have captured your servant. In an hour the sun will set. If you have not delivered yourself to us by that time, we must begin to kill the little fellow. . . ."

Now Hawkmoon knew for certain that it was D'Averc. No other man alive could both look and sound like that. Hawkmoon saw the giant hand the megaphone back to the pilot and then, with the help of his squat companion, help his master to the partially ruined battlement so that D'Averc could lean against it and look down into the streets.

Hawkmoon controlled his fury and studied the distance between his building and the tower. By jumping through the gap in the wall he could reach a series of flat roofs that would take him close to a pile of fallen masonry heaped against one wall of the tower. From there he saw that he could easily climb to the battlements. But he would be seen as soon as he left his cover. It would be possible to take that route only at night—and by nightfall they would have begun torturing Oladahn.

Perplexed, Hawkmoon fingered the black jewel, sign of his former slavery to Granbretan. He knew that if he gave himself up he would be killed instantly or be taken back to Granbretan and there killed with terrible slowness for the pleasure of the perverted lords of the Dark Empire. He thought of Yisselda, to whom he had sworn to return, of Count Brass, whom he had sworn to aid in the struggle against Granbretan—and he thought of Oladahn, with whom he had sworn friendship after the little beast-man had saved his life.

Could he sacrifice his friend? Could he justify such an action, even if logic told him that his own life was of greater worth in the fight against the Dark Empire? Hawkmoon knew that logic was of no use here. But he knew, too, that his sacrifice might be useless, for there was no guarantee that the Boar leader would let Oladahn go once Hawkmoon had delivered himself up.

Hawkmoon bit his lips, gripping his sword tightly; then he came to a decision, squeezed his body through the gap in the wall, clung to the stonework with one hand, and waved his bright blade at the tower. D'Averc looked up slowly.

"You must release Oladahn before I come to you," Hawkmoon called. "For I know that all men of Granbretan are liars. You have *my* word, however, that if you release Oladahn I will deliver myself into your hands."

"Liars we may be," came the languid voice, barely audible, "but we are not fools. How may I trust your word?"

"I am a Duke of Köln," said Hawkmoon simply. "We do not lie."

A light, ironic laugh came from within the boar mask. "You may be naïve, Duke of Köln, but Sir Huillam d'Averc is not. However, may I suggest a compromise?"

"What is that?" Hawkmoon asked warily.

"I would suggest you come halfway toward us so that you are well within the range of our ornithopter's flame-lance, and then I shall release your servant." D'Averc coughed ostentatiously and leaned heavily on the battlement. "What say you to that?"

"Hardly a compromise," called Hawkmoon. "For then you could kill us both with little effort or danger to yourself."

"My dear duke, the King-Emperor would much prefer you alive. Surely you know that? My *own* interest is at stake. Killing you now would only earn me a baronetcy at most—delivering you alive for the King-Emperor's pleasure would almost certainly gain me a princedom. Have you not heard of me, Duke Dorian? I am the *ambitious* Huillam d'Averc."

D'Averc's argument was convincing, but Hawkmoon could not forget the Frenchman's reputation for deviousness. Although it was true that he was worth more to D'Averc alive, the renegade might well decide it expedient not to risk his gains and might therefore kill

Hawkmoon as soon as he came into certain range of the flame-lance.

Hawkmoon deliberated for a moment, then sighed. "I will do as you suggest, Sir Huillam." He poised himself to leap across the narrow street separating him from the rooftops below.

Then Oladahn cried, "No, Duke Dorian! Let them kill me! My life is worthless!"

Hawkmoon acted as if he had not heard his friend and sprang out and down, to land on the balls of his feet on the roof. The old mansonry shuddered at the impact, and for a moment Hawkmoon thought he would fall as the roof threatened to crack. But it held, and he began to walk gingerly toward the tower.

Again Oladahn called out and began to struggle in the hands of his captors.

Hawkmoon ignored him, walking steadily on, sword still in one hand but held loosely, virtually forgotten.

Now Oladahn broke free altogether and darted across the tower, pursued by two cursing warriors. Hawkmoon saw him dash to the far edge, pause for a moment, and then fling himself over the parapet.

For a moment Hawkmoon stood frozen in horror, hardly understanding the nature of his friend's sacrifice.

Then he tightened his grip on his sword and raised his head to glare at D'Averc and his men. Bending low, he made for the edge of the roof as the flame cannon began to turn in his direction. There was a great *whoosh* of heat over his head as they sought his range; then he had swung himself over the edge and hung by his hands, peering down into the street far below.

There was a series of stone carvings quite close to him on his left. He inched along until he could grasp the nearest. They ran down the side of the house at an angle, almost to street level. But the stone was plainly rotten. Would the carvings support his weight?

Hawkmoon did not pause. He swung himself down on the first carving. It began to creak and crumble, like a bad tooth. Quickly Hawkmoon dropped to the next and then the next, bits of stone clattering down the sides of the building, to crash in the distant street.

Then at last Hawkmoon was able to leap to the cobbles and land easily in the soft dust that covered them. Now he began to run, not away from the tower—but toward it. He had nothing in his mind but vengeance on D'Averc for driving Oladahn to suicide.

He found the entrance to the tower and entered in time to hear the clatter of metal-shod feet as D'Averc and his warriors descended. He chose a spot on the staircase (which was enclosed) where he would be able to take the Granbretanians one at a time. D'Averc was the first to appear, stopping suddenly as he saw the glowering Hawkmoon, then reaching with gauntleted hand for his long blade.

"You were foolish not to take the chance of escape your friend's silly sacrifice gave you," said the boar-masked mercenary contemptuously. "Now, like it or not, I suppose we shall have to kill you . . . ." He began to cough, doubling up in apparent agony, leaning weakly against the wall. He signed limply to the squat man behind him—one of those Hawkmoon had seen helping D'Averc across the battlements. "Oh, my dear Duke Dorian, I must apologize . . . my infirmity is liable to seize me at the most inconvenient moments. Ecardo—would you . . . ?"

The powerfully built Ecardo sprang forward grunting and pulling a short-hafted battle-axe from his belt. He tugged out his sword with his free hand and chuckled with pleasure. "Thanks, master. Now let's see how the no-mask prances." He moved like a cat to the attack.

Hawkmoon poised himself, ready to meet Ecardo's first blow.

Then the man sprang with a great feral howl, the battle-axe splashing the air to clang against Hawkmoon's blade. Then Ecardo's short sword ripped upward, and Hawkmoon, already weak from exposure and hunger, barely managed to turn his body in time.

Even so, the sword slashed through the cotton of his britches and he felt its cold edge against his flesh.

Hawkmoon's own blade slid from beneath the axe and crashed down on Ecardo's grinning boar-mask, wrenching one tusk loose and badly denting the snout. Ecardo cursed, his sword stabbing again, but Hawkmoon leaned against the man's sword arm, trapping it beneath his body and the wall. Then he let go of his own sword so that it hung by its wrist thong, grasped Ecardo's arm, and tried to twist the axe from his hand.

Ecardo's armoured knee drove into Hawkmoon's groin, but Hawkmoon held his position in spite of the pain, tugged Ecardo down the stairs, pushed, and let him fall to the floor under his own momentum.

Ecardo hit the paving stones with a thud that shook the whole tower. He did not move.

Hawkmoon looked up at D'Averc. "Well, sir, are you recovered?"

D'Averc pushed back his ornate mask, to reveal the pale face and pale eyes of an invalid. His mouth twisted in a little smile. "I will do my best," he said. And when he advanced it was swiftly, with the movements of a man more than ordinarily fit.

This time Hawkmoon claimed the initiative, darting a thrust at his enemy that almost took him by surprise but that he parried with amazing speed. His languid tone belied his reflexes.

Hawkmoon realized that D'Averc was quite as dangerous, in his own way, as the powerful Ecardo. He realized, too, that if Ecardo were merely stunned, he himself might soon be trapped between two opponents.

The swordplay was so swift that the two blades seemed a single blur of metal as both men held their ground. With his greast mask flung back, D'Averc was smiling, with an expression of quiet pleasure in his eyes. He looked for all the world like a man enjoying a musical performance or some other passive pastime.

Wearied by his journey through the desert, needing food, Hawkmoon knew that he could not long sustain the fight in this way. Desperately he sought an opening in D'Averc's splendid defense. Once, his opponent stumbled slightly on a broken stair. Hawkmoon thrust swiftly but was parried and had his forearm nicked into the bargain.

Behind D'Averc the warriors of the Boar waited eagerly with swords ready to finish Hawkmoon off once the opportunity was presented to them.

Hawkmoon was tiring rapidly until he was fighting a purely defensive style, barely managing to turn the thrusting steel that drove for his eye, his throat, his heart, or his belly. He took one step backward, then another.

As he took the second step, he heard a groan behind him and knew that Ecardo's senses were returning. It would not be long before the boars butchered him.

Yet he scarcely cared, now that Oladahn was dead. Hawkmoon's swordplay became wilder, and D'Averc's smile grew broader as he sensed his victory coming closer.

Rather than have Ecardo at his back, Hawkmoon sprang suddenly down the steps without turning around. His shoulder bumped against another, and he whirled, prepared to face the brutish Ecardo.

Then his sword almost dropped from his hand in astonishment.

"Oladahn!"

The little beast-man was in the act of raising a sword—the boar warrior's own sword—over the stirring Ecardo's head.

"Aye—I live. But do not ask me how. It's a mystery to me." And he brought the flat of the blade down on Ecardo's helmet with a great clang. Ecardo collapsed again.

There was no more time for talk. Hawkmoon barely managed to block D'Averc's next thrust. There was a look of astonishment in D'Averc's eyes too as he saw the living Oladahn.

Hawkmoon managed to break through the Frenchman's guard, piercing his shoulder armour. Again D'Averc swept the blade aside and resumed the attack. Hawkmoon had lost the advantage of his position. The savage boar mask grinned at him as warriors poured down the stairs.

Hawkmoon and Oladahn backed toward the door, hoping to regain the advantage, but there was little chance of that. For another ten minutes they held their own against the over-whelming odds, killing two Granbretanians, wounding three more. They were wearying rapidly. Hawkmoon could barely hold his sword.

His glazed eyes tried to focus on his opponents as they closed in like brutes for the kill. He heard D'Averc's triumphant 'Take them alive!' and then he went down beneath a tide of metal.

Chapter Three

THE WRAITH-FOLK

WRAPPED IN CHAINS so that they could barely breathe, Hawkmoon and Oladahn were borne down innumerable flights of stairs into the depths of the great tower, which seemed to stretch as far below ground as it did above.

At length the boar warriors reached a chamber that had evidently been a storeroom but which now served as an effective dungeon.

There they were flung face down on the coarse rock. They lay there until a booted foot turned them over to blink into the light of a guttering torch held by the squat Ecardo, whose battered mask seemed to snarl in glee. D'Averc, mask still pushed back to expose his face, stood between Ecardo and the huge, hairy warrior Hawkmoon had seen earlier. D'Averc had a brocade scarf to his lips, and he leaned heavily on the giant's arm.

D'Averc coughed musically and smiled down at his prisoners. "I fear I must leave you soon, gentlemen. This subterranean air is not good for me. However, it should do little harm to two such robust young fellows as yourselves. You will not have to stay here more than a day, I assure you. I have sent a request for a larger ornithopter that will be able to bear the two of you back to Sicilia, where my main force is now encamped."

"You have taken Sicilia already?" Hawkmoon asked tonelessly. "You have conquered the isle?"

"Aye. The Dark Empire wastes little time. I, in fact" —D'Averc coughed with mock modesty into his scarf — "am the *hero* of Sicilia. It was my leadership that subjugated the island so swiftly. But that triumph was no special one, for the Dark Empire has many capable captains like myself. We have made excellent gains in Europe these past few months—and in the East, too."

"But the Kamarg still stands," Hawkmoon said. "That must irritate the King-Emperor."

"Oh, the Kamarg cannot last long besieged," said D'Averc airily. "We are concentrating our *particular* attention on that little province. Why, it may have fallen already. . . ."

"Not while Count Brass lives," Hawkmoon smiled.

"Just so," D'Averc said. "I heard he was badly wounded and his lieutenant von Villach slain in a recent battle."

Hawkmoon could not tell whether D'Averc was lying. He let no emotion show on his face, but the news had shocked him. Was the Kamarg ready to fall—and if so, what would become of Yisselda?

"Plainly that news disturbs *you*," D'Averc murmured. "But fear not, Duke, for when the Kamarg falls it will be in my safekeeping if all goes well. I plan to claim the province as my reward for capturing you. And these, my boon companions," he continued, indicating his brutish servants, "I will elevate to rule the Kamarg when I cannot. They share all aspects of my life—my secrets, my pleasures. It is only fair that they should share my triumph. Ecardo I will make steward of my estates, and I think I shall make Peter here a Count."

From within the giant's mask came an animal grunt. D'Averc smiled. "Peter has few brains, but his strength and his loyalty are without question. Perhaps I'll replace Count Brass with him."

Hawkmoon stirred angrily in his chains. "You are a wily beast, D'Averc, but I will not let you goad me to an outburst, if that's what you desire. I'll bide my time. Perhaps I'll escape you yet. And if I do—you may live in terror for the day when our roles are reversed and you are in *my* power."

"I fear you are too optimistic, Duke. Rest here, enjoy the peace, for you'll know none when you get to Granbretan."

With a mocking bow, D'Averc left, his men following. The torchlight faded, and Hawkmoon and Oladahn were left in darkness.

"Ah," came Oladahn's voice after a while. "I find it difficult to take my position seriously after all that has happened today. I am still not even sure whether this be dream, death, or reality."

"What did happen to you, Oladahn?" Hawkmoon asked. "How could you survive the great leap? I had imagined you dashed to death beneath the tower."

"By rights I should have been," Oladahn agreed. "If I had not been arrested by ghosts in midfall."

"Ghosts? You jest."

"Nay. These things—like ghosts—appeared from windows in the tower and bore me gently to earth. They were the size and shape of men but barely tangible. . . ."

"You fell and knocked your head and dreamed this stuff!"

"You could be right." Suddenly Oladahn paused. "But if so, I am dreaming still. Look to your left."

Hawkmoon turned his head, gasping in astonishment at what he saw. There, quite plainly, he could see the figure of a man. Yet, as if through a pool of milk, he could see *beyond* the man and make out the wall behind him.

"A ghost of a classic sort," Hawkmoon said. "Strange to share a dream. . . ."

Faint, musical laughter came from the figure standing over them. "You do not dream, strangers. We are men like you. The mass of our bodies is merely altered a little, that is all. We do not exist in quite the same dimensions as you. But we are real enough. We are the men of Soryandum."

"So you have not deserted your city," Oladahn said. "But how did you attain this . . . peculiar state of existence."

The wraith-man laughed again. "By control of the mind, scientific experiment, by a certain mastery of time and space. I regret that it would be impossible to describe how we came to this condition, for we reached it, among other ways, by the creation of an entirely new vocabulary, and the language I would use would mean nothing to you. However, be assured of one thing—we are still able to judge human characters well enough and recognize you as potential friends and those others as actual enemies."

"Enemies of yours? How so?" Hawkmoon asked.

"I will explain later." The wraith-man glided forward until he was leaning over Hawkmoon. The young Duke of Köln felt a strange pressure on his body, and then he was lifted up. The man might have looked intangible, but he seemed far stronger than an ordinary mortal. From the shadows two more of the wraith-people drifted, one to pick up Oladahn and the other to raise his hand and somehow produce a radiance in the dungeon that was mellow yet adequate to illuminate the whole place. Hawkmoon saw that the wraith-men were tall and slender, with thin, handsome faces and blind-seeming eyes.

Hawkmoon had supposed at first that the people of Soryandum were able to pass through solid walls, but now he saw that they had entered from above, for there was a large tunnel about halfway up the wall. Perhaps in the distant past this tunnel has been some kind of chute down which sacks of stores had been rolled.

Now the wraith-people rose into the air toward the tunnel and entered it, drifting up it until light could be seen far ahead—the light of moon and stars.

"Where are you taking us?" Hawkmoon whispered.

"To a safer place where we shall be able to free you of your chains," the man who carried him answered.

When they reached the top of the tunnel and felt the chill of the night air, they paused while the one who had no burden went ahead to make sure that there were no Granbretanian warriors about. He signed to the others to follow, and they drifted out into the ruined streets of the silent city until they came to a simple three-storied house that was in better condition than the rest but seemed to have no means of entrance at ground level.

The wraith-folk bore Hawkmoon and Oladahn upward again, to the second level, and passed through a wide window into the house.

In a room bare of any ornamentation they came to rest, setting the pair down gently.

"What is this place?" Hawkmoon asked, still unable to trust his senses.

"This is where we live," the wraith-man replied. "There are not many of us. Though we live for centuries, we are incapable of reproducing ourselves. That is what we lost when we became as we are."

Now through the door came other figures, several of them female. All were of the same beautiful and graceful appearance, all had bodies of milky opaqueness; none wore clothes. The faces and bodies were ageless, scarcely human, but they radiated such a sense of tranquility that Hawkmoon immediately felt relaxed and secure.

One of the newcomers had brought with him a small instrument, scarcely larger than Hawkmoon's index finger, which he now applied to the several padlocks on the chains. One by one the locks sprang open, until at last Hawkmoon and then Oladahn were free.

Hawkmoon sat up, rubbing at his aching muscles. "I thank you," he said. "You have saved me from an unpleasant fate."

"We are happy to have been of use,". replied one of their number, slightly shorter than the rest. "I am Rinal, once Chief Councillor of Soryandum." He came forward smiling. "And we wonder if it would interest you that you could be of help to us, also."

"I would be glad to perform any service in repayment of what you have done for me," Hawkmoon said earnestly. "What is it?"

"We, too, are in great danger from those strange warriors with their grotesque beast-masks," Rinal told him. "For they plan to raze Soryandum."

"Raze it? But why? This city offers no threat to them—and it is too remote to be worth their annexing."

"Not so," Rinal said. "For we have listened to their conversations and know that Soryandum is of value to them. They wish to build a great structure here that will house scores and hundreds of their flying machines. The machines can then be sent out to all the surrounding lands to threaten and defeat them."

"I understand," Hawkmoon murmured. "It makes sense. And that is why D'Averc, the ex-architect, was chosen for this particular mission. Building materials already exist here and could be remodeled to form one of their ornithopter bases, and the spot is so remote that few, if any, would note the activity. The Dark Empire would have surprise on their side right up to the moment they wished to launch an attack. They must be stopped!"

"They must be, if only for our sake," Rinal continued. "You see, we are part of this city perhaps more than you can understand. It and we exist as the same thing. If the city were destroyed, we should perish also."

"But how can we stop them?" Hawkmoon said. "And how can I be of use? You must have the resources of a sophisticated science at your disposal. I have only a sword—and even that is in the hands of D'Averc!"

"I told you that we are linked to the city," Rinal said patiently. "And that is exactly the case. We cannot move away from the city. Long ago we rid ourselves of such unsubtle things as machines. They were buried under a hillside many miles from Soryandum. Now we have need for one particular machine, and we cannot ourselves obtain it. You, however, with your mortal mobility, could get it for us."

"Willingly," said Hawkmoon. "If you give us the exact location of the machine we shall bring it to you. Best if we left soon, before D'Averc realizes we have escaped."

"I agree that the thing should be accomplished as soon as possible," Rinal nodded, "but I have omitted to tell you one thing. The machines were placed there by us while we were still able to make short journeys away from Soryandum. To make sure that they were not disturbed, we protected them with a beast-machine—a dreadful contraption designed to frighten off whoever should discover the store. But the metal creature can also kill—will kill any not of our race who dares enter the cavern."

"Then how may we nullify this beast?" Oladahn asked.

"There is but one way for you," Rinal said with a sigh. "You must fight it—and destroy it."

"I see." Hawkmoon smiled. "So I escaped from one predicament to face another scarcely less dangerous."

Rinal raised his hand. "No. We make no demands

on you. If you feel that your life would be more useful in the service of some other cause, forget us at once and go your way."

"I owe you my life," Hawkmoon said. "And my conscience would not be clear if I rode away from Soryandum knowing that your city would be destroyed, your race exterminated, and the Dark Empire given the opportunity to wreak even more havoc in the East than it has already. No—I will do what I can, though without weapons it will not be an easy task."

Rinal signed to one of the wraith-folk, who drifted from the room, to return at length with Hawkmoon's battered battle-blade and Oladahn's bow, arrows, and sword. "We found it an easy matter to recover these," smiled Rinal. "And we have another weapon, of sorts, for you." He handed Hawkmoon the tiny device they had used earlier to open the padlocks. "This we retained when we put most of our other machines in store. It is capable of opening any lock—all you must do is point at it. It will help you gain entrance to the main storeroom where the mechanical beast guards the old machines of Soryandum."

"And what is the machine you desire us to find?" Oladahn asked.

"It is a small device, about the size of a man's head. Its colors are those of the rainbow, and it shines. It looks like crystal but feels like metal. It has a base of onyx, and from this projects an octagonal object. There may be two in the storeroom. If you can, bring both."

"What does it do?" Hawkmoon inquired.

"That you will see when you return with it."

"If we return with it," said Oladahn in a tone of philosophical gloom.

Chapter Four

THE MECHANICAL BEAST

HAVING REFRESHED THEMSELVES on food and wine stolen from D'Averc's men by the wraith-folk, Hawkmoon and Oladahn strapped on their weapons and prepared to leave the house.

With two of the men of Soryandum supporting them, they were borne gently down to the ground.

"May the Runestaff protect you," whispered one, as the pair made for the city wall, "for we have heard that you serve it."

Hawkmoon turned to ask him how he had heard this. It was the second time he had been told that he served the Runestaff; yet he had no knowledge that he did. But before he could speak the wraith-man had vanished.

Frowning, Hawkmoon led the way from the city.

* * *

Deep in the hills several miles from Soryandum, Hawkmoon paused to get his bearings. Rinal had told him to look for a cairn out of cut granite, left there centuries before by Rinal's ancestors. At last he saw it, old stone turned to silver by the moonlight.

"Now we go north," he said, "and look for the hill from which the granite was cut."

Another half hour and they made out the hill. It looked as if at some time a giant sword had sliced its face sheer. Since that time grass had grown over it again so that the characteristic seemed a natural one.

Hawkmoon and Oladahn crossed springy turf to a place where thick shrubs grew against the side of the hill. Parting these, they discerned a narrow opening in the cliffside. This was the secret entrance to the machine stores of the people of Soryandum.

Squeezing through the entrance, the two men found themselves in a large cave. Oladahn lit the brand they had brought for the purpose, and the flickering light revealed a great, square cavern that had evidently been hewn artificially.

Remembering his instructions, Hawkmoon crossed to the far wall of the cave and looked for a tiny mark at shoulder height. At last he saw it—a sign written in unfamiliar characters, and beneath it a tiny hole. Hawkmoon took from his shirt the instrument they had been given and pointed it at the hole.

He felt a tingling sensation in his hand as he applied slight pressure to the instrument. The rock before him began to tremble. A powerful gust of air made the brand flames stream, threatening to blow them out. The wall began to glow, become transparent, and then disappear altogether. "It will still be there," Rinal had told them, "but temporarily removed to another dimension."

Cautiously, swords in hand, they passed through into a great tunnel full of cool, green light from walls like fused glass.

Ahead of them lay another wall. On it glowed a single red spot, and it was at this that Hawkmoon now pointed the instrument.

Again there was a sudden rush of air. This time it nearly blew them over. Then the wall glowed white, turning to a milky blue before vanishing altogether.

This section of the tunnel was the same milky-blue colour, but the wall ahead of them was black. When it, too, had faded, they entered a tunnel of yellow stone and knew that the main store chamber and its guardian lay ahead of them.

Hawkmoon paused before applying the instrument to the white wall they faced.

"We must be cunning and move swiftly," he told Oladahn, "for the creature beyond this wall will come alive the moment it senses our presence—"

He broke off as a muffled sound reached their ears

—a fantastic clashing and clattering. The white wall shuddered as if something on the other side had flung a huge weight against it.

Oladahn looked dubiously at the wall. "Perhaps we should reconsider. After all, if we wasted our lives uselessly we . . ."

But Hawkmoon was already activating the instrument, and the protecting wall had begun to change colour as the strange, cold wind struck their faces. From behind the wall came an awesome wail of pain and bewilderment. The walls turned to pink, faded—and revealed the machine-beast.

The wall's disappearance seemed to have disturbed it for an instant, for it made no move toward them. It crouched on metal feet, towering over them, its multicolored scales half-blinding them. The length of its back, save for its neck, was a mass of knife-sharp horns. It had a body fashioned somewhat like an ape's, with short hind legs and long forelegs ending in hands of taloned metal. Its eyes were multifaceted like a fly's, glowing with shifting colours, and its snout was full of razor-sharp metal teeth.

Beyond the mechanical beast they could see great heaps of machinery, stacked in orderly rows about the walls. The room was vast. Somewhere in the middle of it, on his left, Hawkmoon saw the two crystalline devices Rinal had described. Silently, he pointed to them, then made to dash past the monster, into the storeroom.

Their movements as they ran stirred the beast from its daze. It screamed and lumbered after them, exuding a repulsive metallic smell.

From the corner of his eye Hawkmoon saw a gigantic taloned hand clutching at him. He swerved aside, knocking into a delicate machine that toppled and smashed to the floor, scattering bits of glass and broken metal parts. The hand plucked at air an inch from his face, then grabbed again, but Hawkmoon had already sidestepped.

An arrow suddenly struck the beast's snout with a

clatter of metal on metal, but it did not scratch the yellow and black scales.

With a roar, the beast sought its other enemy, saw Oladahn, and pounced toward him.

Oladahn scampered backward but not fast enough, for the creature seized him in its paw and drew him towards its gaping mouth. Hawkmoon yelled and struck his sword at the thing's groin. It snorted and flung its prisoner aside Oladahn lay supine in a corner by the door, either stunned or slain.

Hawkmoon backed away as the creature advanced; then he suddenly changed tactics, ducked, and dashed between the surprised beast's legs. As it began to turn, Hawkmoon dashed back again.

The metal monster snorted in fury, its claws thrashing about it. It leaped into the air and came down with an earsplitting crash, rushing across the floor of the gallery at Hawkmoon, who squeezed down between two machines and, using them for cover, crept closer to the machines he had come to take.

Now the monster began to wrench machines aside in its insensate search for its enemy. Hawkmoon came to a stop by a machine with a bell-shaped nozzle. At the end of his nozzle was a lever. The machine seemed to be some kind of weapon. Without pausing to think, Hawkmoon pulled the lever. A faint noise came from the thing, but nothing else seemed to result.

Now the beast was almost upon him again.

Hawkmoon prepared to make a stand, deciding that he would fling his sword at one of the eyes, since they seemed to be the creature's most vulnerable feature. Rinal had told him that the mechanical beast could not be killed in any ordinary sense; but if it were blinded, he might stand a chance.

But now, as the beast came into direct line of the machine, it staggered and grunted. Evidently some invisible ray was attacking it, possibly interfering with its complicated mechanism. It staggered, and Hawkmoon felt triumphant for an instant, judging the beast defeated. But the creature shook its body and began to advance again with slow, painful movements.

Hawkmoon saw that it was slowly regaining its strength. He must strike now if he was to have any chance at all. He ran toward the beast. It turned its head slowly. But then Hawkmoon had leaped at its squat neck and was climbing up the scales to seat himself on the mechanical beast's shoulders. With a growl it raised its arm to tear Hawkmoon away.

Desperately Hawkmoon leaned forward and with the pommel of his sword struck first at one eye and then at the other. With a sharp, splintering sound, both eyes were dashed to fragments.

The beast screamed, its paws going not to Hawkmoon but to its injured eyes, giving the young Duke time to leap from the creature's back and dash for the two boxes he sought.

He pulled a sack from where it was looped over his belt and dropped the two boxes into it.

The mechanical monster was flailing around. Metal buckled and snapped wherever it struck. Blind it might now be, but it had lost none of its strength.

Skipping around the screaming beast, Hawkmoon ran to where Oladahn lay, bundled the little man over his shoulder, and ran for the exit.

Behind him the metal beast had caught the sound of his footsteps and had begun to turn in pursuit, Hawkmoon increased his pace, his heart seeming about to burst from his ribcage with the effort.

Down the corridors he raced, one after the other, until he reached the cave and the narrow opening that led to the outside world. The metal monster would not be able to follow him through such a tiny crack.

As soon as he squeezed through the opening and felt the night air in his lungs, he relaxed and studied Oladahn's face. The little beast-man was breathing well enough, and there seemed to be nothing broken. Only a livid bruise on his head seemed serious, explaining why he was unconscious. Even as he inspected Oladahn's body, for worse injuries, the beast-man's eyes began to flutter open. A faint sound came from his lips.

"Oladahn, are you all right?" Hawkmoon asked anxiously.

"Ugh—my head's on fire," Oladahn grunted. "Where are we?"

"Safe. Now try to rise. Dawn is almost here, and we must get back to Soryandum before morning, or D'Averc's men will see us."

Painfully Oladahn pulled himself to his feet. From within the cave came a wild howling and thundering as the mechanical beast sought to reach them.

"Safe?" Oladahn said, pointing to the hillside behind Hawkmoon. "Possibly—but for how long?"

Hawkmoon turned. A great fissure had appeared in the cliff face as the mechanical beast strove to free itself and follow its enemies.

"All the more need for speed," said Hawkmoon, picking up his bundle and beginning to run back in the direction of Soryandum.

They had not gone half a mile before they heard an enormous crash behind them. Looking back, they saw the face of the hill split open and the metal beast emerge, its howling echoing through the hills, threatening to reach all the way to Soryandum.

"The beast is blind," Hawkmoon explained, "so it may not follow us at once. Perhaps if we can reach the city we will be safe from it."

They increased their pace and were soon on the outskirts of Soryandum.

Not much later, as dawn came, they were creeping through the streets seeking the house of the wraith-folk.

Chapter Five

THE MACHINE

RINAL AND TWO others met them by the house and hastily bore them up to the entrance window. As the sun rose and light fell through the windows, making the wraith-folk look even less tangible than before, Rinal eagerly took the boxes from Hawkmoon's sack.

"They are as I remember," he murmured, his strange body drifting into the light so that he might look at the objects better. His ghostly hand stroked the octagon set in its onyx base. "Now we need have no fear of the masked strangers. We can escape from them whenever we please. . . ."

"But I thought there was *no* way for you to leave the city," Oladahn said.

"That is true—but with these machines, we can take the whole city with us, if we are lucky."

Hawkmoon was about to question Rinal further, when he heard a commotion in the street outside and sidled to the window to peer cautiously down. There he saw D'Averc, his two brutish lieutenants, and about twenty warriors. One of the warriors was pointing up at the window.

"We have been seen," Hawkmoon said. "We must all leave. We cannot fight so many."

Rinal frowned. "We cannot leave, either. But if we use our machine, it will put you at D'Averc's mercy. I am in a dilemma."

"Use the machine then," Hawkmoon said, "and let us worry about D'Averc."

"We cannot let you die for our sakes! Not after all you have done."

"Use the machine!"

But Rinal still hesitated.

Hawkmoon heard another sound outside and glanced cautiously through the window. "They've brought up ladders. They're about to enter. Use the machine, Rinal."

Another of the wraith-folk, a woman said softly, "Use the machine, Rinal. If what we heard was true, then it is unlikely that our friend will come to much harm at D'Averc's hands, not at this moment, anyway."

"What do you mean?" Hawkmoon asked. "How do you know this?"

"We have a friend not of our people," the woman told him, "who sometimes visits us, bringing us news of the outside world. He, too, serves the Runestaff—"

"Is he a warrior in armour of jet and gold?" Hawkmoon interrupted.

"Aye, he told us you—"

"Duke Dorian!" Oladahn cried, pointing to the window. The first of the boar warriors had reached the window.

Hawkmoon whipped his sword from the scabbard, leaped forward, and drove the blade into the throat of the warrior just below his gorget. The man went backward and down with a gurgling scream. Hawkmoon seized the ladder, trying to twist it aside. It was firmly held below. Another warrior came level with the window, and Oladahn swung at his head knocking him sideways, but the man clung on. Hawkmoon relinquished his hold on the ladder and hacked at the man's gauntleted fingers. With a yell he let go and crashed to the ground.

"The machine," Hawkmoon called desperately. "Use it, Rinal. We cannot hold them for long."

From behind him there came a musical thrumming sound, and Hawkmoon felt slightly dizzy as his sword met that of the next attacker.

Then everything began to vibrate rapidly, and the walls of the house turned bright red. Outside in the street the boar warriors were yelling—not in surprise, but in outright fear. Hawkmoon could not understand why the sight terrified them so much.

He could see now that the whole city had turned the same vibrating scarlet and seemed to be shaking itself to pieces in harmony with the thrumming of the machine. Then, abruptly, sound and city vanished and Hawkmoon was falling gently earthward.

He heard the voice of Rinal, faint and disappearing, say, "We have left you the twin of this machine. It is our gift to aid you against your enemies. It has the ability to shift whole areas of the earth into a slightly different dimension of space-time. Our enemies will not have Soryandum now. . . ."

Then Hawkmoon landed on rocky ground, Oladahn close by, and saw that there was not a trace of the city. Instead there was pitted ground that looked as if it had recently been plowed.

Some distance away were the troops of Granbretan, D'Averc among them, and Hawkmoon could see now why they had screamed in terror.

The machine beast had come at last to the city and was attacking the boar warriors. Everywhere were the battered and bleeding corpses of Granbretanians. Urged on by D'Averc, who had his own sword drawn and was joining them in the battle, the Granbretanians were trying to destroy the monster.

Its metal spines shook in fury, its metal teeth clashed in its head, and its metal talons ripped and rended armour and flesh.

"The beast will take care of them," Hawkmoon said. "Look—our horses." About three hundred yards away stood the two bewildered steeds. Hawkmoon and Oladahn ran for them and were soon mounted, riding away from the site of Soryandum and the carnage that the mechanical beast was making of D'Averc's boars.

Now, with the strange gift of the wraith-folk wrapped carefully and placed in Hawkmoon's saddlebag, the two adventurers continued their journey to the coast.

The coarse turf was easier on the horses' hooves, and they made rapid progress over the hills until they came at last to the wide valley where the Euphrates flowed.

By the banks of the broad river they made their camp and debated how best to cross, for the water was fast-flowing at this stretch, and according to Hawkmoon's map, they would have to journey several miles south before they came to a likely fording place.

Hawkmoon stared across the water as the setting sun stained it the colour of poppies. A long, almost silent sigh escaped him, and Oladahn looked up curiously from where he was laying the fire.

"What troubles you, Duke Dorian? One would have thought you in good spirits after our escape."

"It is the future that troubles me, Oladahn. If D'Averc were right and Count Brass lies wounded, with von Villach dead and the Kamarg under powerful siege, then I fear we shall return to find nothing but the ashes and mud Baron Meliadus once promised he would make of the Kamarg."

"Let us wait until we get there," Oladahn said with attempted cheerfulness, "for it is likely that D'Averc only sought to make you gloomy. Almost certainly your Kamarg still stands. From all you have told me of the great defences and the mighty valor of the province, I do not doubt that they still hold against the Dark Empire. You will see. . . ."

"But will I?" Hawkmoon's gaze dropped to the darkening ground. "Will I, Oladahn? D'Averc was almost certainly right when he spoke of Granbretan's other conquests. If Sicilia is theirs, then so must be parts of Italia and Espanyia. Don't you see what that means?"

"Outside of the Bulgar mountains my geography is weak," Oladahn said embarrassedly.

"It means that all routes to the Kamarg—by both land and sea—are blocked by the Dark Empire's hordes. Even if we reach the sea and find a ship, what chance will we have of passing unharmed through the Sicilian Channel? The waters there must be thick with Dark Empire ships."

"But do we have to travel that way? What about the route you used to reach the East?"

Hawkmoon frowned. "Much of that territory I flew across, and it would take twice the time to go back that way. Also Granbretan has already made extra gains there."

"But the territories under their control could be circumnavigated," Oladahn said. "At least on land we should stand some chance, while on sea, from what you say, no chance at all."

"Aye," said Hawkmoon thoughtfully. "But it would mean crossing Turkia—a journey of several weeks. But then, perhaps, we could use the Black Sea, which, I hear, is fairly free of Dark Empire ships still." He consulted the map. "Aye—the Black Sea across to Romania—but then it would become increasingly dangerous as we neared France, for the Dark Empire's forces are everywhere thereabouts. Still, you are right—we would have a better chance by that route; might even slay a couple of Granbretanians and use their masks as disguises. One disadvantage that they have is that their faces cannot be recognized as those of friend or foe. If it were not for the secret languages of the various orders, we could travel safely enough if tricked out in beast masks and armor."

"Then we change our route," Oladahn said.

"Yes. We go north in the morning."

For a number of long days they followed the Euphrates north, crossing the borders between Syria and Turkia and coming at length to the quiet white town of Birachek, where the Euphrates became the Firat River.

In Birachek a wary innkeeper, suspecting them as servants of the Dark Empire, told them at first that there were no rooms, but then Hawkmoon pointed to the black jewel in his forehead and said, "My name is Dorian, last Duke of Köln, sworn enemy of Granbretan," and the innkeeper, even in this remote town, had heard of him and let them in.

Later that night they sat in the public room of the inn, drinking sweet wine and talking to the members of a trading caravan that had arrived in Birachek shortly before them.

The traders were swarthy men with blue-black hair and beards that gleamed with oil. They were dressed in leather shirts and brightly colored divided kilts of wool; over these clothes they wore woven cloaks, also of wool, in geometric designs of purple, red, and yellow. These cloaks, they told the travelers, showed that they were the men of Yenahan, merchant of Ankara. At their waists were curved sabres with richly decorated hilts and engraved blades, worn unscabbarded. These traders were as used to fighting as they were to bartering.

Their leader, Saleem, hawk-nosed and with piercing blue eyes, leaned forward over the table to speak slowly to the Duke of Köln and Oladahn.

"You have heard that emissaries of the Dark Empire pay court to the Calif of Istanbul and bribe that thriftless monarch to let them station a large force of bull-masked warriors within the city walls?"

Hawkmoon shook his head. "I have little news of the world. But I believe you. It is the way of Granbretan to take with gold rather than take with force. Only if gold is no longer of use will they produce their weapons and armies."

Saleem nodded. "As I thought. You would not, then, think Turkia safe from the Western wolves?"

"Not any part of the world, even Amarehk, is safe from their ambition. They dream of conquering lands that might not even exist, save in fables. They plan to take Asiacommunista, though they must find it first.

Arabia and the East are mere camping grounds for their armies."

"But could they have such power?" Saleem asked, astonished.

"They have the power," Hawkmoon said with confidence. "They have a madness, too, which makes them savage, cunning—and inventive. I have seen Londra, capital of Granbretan, and its vast architecture is that of brilliant nightmares made solid. I have seen the King-Emperor himself in his throne globe of milky fluid—a wizened immortal with the golden voice of a youth. I have seen the laboratories of the sorcerer-scientists—innumerable caverns of bizarre machines, many whose functions have yet to be rediscovered by the Granbretanians themselves. And I have talked with their nobles, learned of their ambitions, know them to be more insane than anything you or any other normal man could imagine. They are without humanity, have little feeling for each other and none at all for those they regard as lower species—that is, all those not of Granbretan. They crucify men, women, children, and animals to decorate and mark the roads to and from their conquests. . . ."

Saleem leaned back with a wave of his hand. "Ah, come now, Duke Dorian, you exaggerate. . . ."

Hawkmoon said forcefully, glaring into Saleem's eyes, "I tell you this, trader of Turkia—I *cannot* exaggerate the evil of Granbretan!"

Saleem frowned then and shuddered. "I—I believe you," he said. "But I wish that I could not. For how can the little nation of Turkia withstand such might and cruelty?"

Hawkmoon sighed. "I can offer no solution. I would say that you should band together, do not let them weaken you with gold and gradual encroachment in your lands—but I would waste my rhetoric if I tried, for men are greedy and will not see the truth for the gleam of coin. Resist them, I would say, with honour and honest courage, with wisdom and with idealism.

Yet those who resist them are vanquished and tortured, see their wives raped and torn apart before their eyes, their children become playthings of warriors and heaped on fires lit to burn whole cities. But if you do not resist, if you escape death in battle, then the same could still happen to you, or you and yours become cringing things, less than human, willing to perform any indignity, any act of evil, to save your skins. I spoke of honesty—and honesty forbids me to encourage you with brave talk of noble battle and warriors' deaths. I seek to destroy them—I am their declared enemy—but I have great allies and considerable luck, and even I feel that I cannot forever escape their vengeance, though I have done so several times. I can only advise those who would have something to resist the minions of King Huon—use cunning. Use cunning, my friend. It is the only weapon we have against the Dark Empire."

"Pretend to serve them, you mean?" Saleem said thoughtfully.

"I did so. I am alive now and comparatively free . . ."

"I will remember your words, westerner."

"Remember them *all*," Hawkmoon warned him. "For the hardest compromise to make is when you decide to *appear* to compromise. Often the deception becomes the reality long before you realize it."

Saleem fingered his beard. "I understand you." He glanced about the room. The flickering shadows of the torches seemed to take on a sudden menace. "How long, I wonder, will it be? . . . So much of Europe is already theirs."

"Have you heard anything of the province called the Kamarg?" asked Hawkmoon.

"The Kamarg. A land of horned werebeasts, is it not, and half-human monsters with mighty powers, who have somehow managed to stand against the Dark Empire. They are led by a metal giant, the Brass Count . . ."

Hawkmoon smiled. "You have heard much that is legend. Count Brass is flesh and blood, and there are few monsters in the Kamarg. The only horned beasts are the bulls of the marshlands and the horses, too. And have they still resisted the Dark Empire? Heard you of how Count Brass fares, or his lieutenant von Villach—or Count Brass's daughter, Yisselda"

"I heard Count Brass dead and his lieutenant, too. But of a girl I heard nothing—and as far as I know the Kamarg still stands."

Hawkmoon rubbed at the black jewel. "Your information is not certain enough. I cannot believe that if Count Brass is dead the Kamarg still stands. If Count Brass goes down, so does the province."

"Well, I speak only of rumors surrounding other rumors," Saleen said. "We traders are sure of local gossip, but most of what we hear of the West is vague and obscure. You come from the Kamarg, do you not?"

"It is my adopted home," Hawkmoon agreed. "If it still exists."

Oladahn put his hand on Hawkmoon's shoulder. "Do not be depressed, Duke Dorian. You said yourself that Trader Saleem's information is barely credible. Wait until we are nearer our goal before you lose hope."

Hawkmoon made an effort to rid himself of the mood, calling for more wine and plates of broiled pieces of mutton and hot unleavened bread. And although he was able to appear more cheerful, his mind was not at rest for fear that all those he loved were indeed dead and the wild beauty of the Kamarg marshlands now turned to a burning waste.

Chapter Six

MAD GOD'S SHIP

TRAVELLING WITH SALEEM and his traders to Ankara and thence to the port of Zonguldak on the Black Sea, Hawkmoon and Oladahn were able, with the help of papers supplied by Saleem's master, to get passage on board the *Smiling Girl,* the only ship ready to take them with it to Simferopol on the coast of a land called Crimia. *Smiling Girl* was not a pretty vessel, and neither did she seem happy. Captain and crew were filthy, and the decks below stank of a thousand different kinds of rot. Yet they were forced to pay heavily for the privilege of passage on the tub, and their quarters were little less noxious than the bilges over which they were positioned. Captain Mouso, with his long, greasy moustachios and shifty eyes, did not inspire their confidence, and neither did the bottle of strong wine that seemed permanently in the mate's hairy paw.

Philosophically, Hawkmoon decided that at least the ship would hardly be worth a pirate's attention—and, for the same reason, a Dark Empire ship's attention—and went aboard with Oladahn shortly before she sailed.

Smiling Girl lumbered away from the quayside on the early-morning tide. As her patched sails caught the wind, every timber in her groaned and creaked; she turned sluggishly north northeast under a darkening sky that was full of rain. The morning was cool and gray, with a peculiar muted quality to it that dampened sounds and made seeing an effort.

Huddled in his cloak, Hawkmoon stood in the fo'c'sle and watched as Zonguldak disappeared behind them.

Rain had begun to fall in heavy drops by the time the port was out of sight and Oladahn came up from below to move along the heaving deck toward Hawkmoon.

"I've cleaned up our quarters as best I can, Duke Dorian, though we'll not be free of the smell from the rest of the ship—and there's little, I'd guess, that would scare away such fat rats as I saw."

"We'll bear it," Hawkmoon said stoically. "We've borne worse, and the voyage is only for two days." He glanced at the mate, who was reeling out of the wheelhouse. "Though I'd be happier if I thought the ship's officers and crew were a trifle more capable." He smiled. "If the mate drinks any more and the captain lies snoring much longer, we may find ourselves with a command!"

Rather than go below, the two men stood together in the rain, looking to the north and wondering what might befall them on their long journey to the Kamarg.

The miserable ship sailed on through the miserable day, tossed on the rough sea, blown by a treacherous wind that ever threatened to become a storm but always stopped just short. The captain stumbled onto the bridge from time to time, to shout at his men, to curse them and beat them into the rigging to reef that sail or loose another. To Hawkmoon and Oladahn, Captain Mouso's orders seemed entirely arbitrary.

Toward evening, Hawkmoon went to join the Captain on the bridge. Mouso looked up at him with a shifty expression.

"Good evening, sir," he said, sniffing and wiping his long nose with his sleeve. "I hope the voyage's to your satisfaction."

"Reasonably, thank you. What time have we made—good or bad?"

"Good enough, sir," replied the skipper, turning so that he did not have to look at Hawkmoon directly. "Good enough. Shall I have the galley prepare you some supper?"

Hawkmoon nodded. "Aye."

The mate appeared from below the bridge, singing softly to himself and evidently blind drunk.

Now a sudden squall hit the ship side on, and the ship wallowed over alarmingly. Hawkmoon clung to the rail, feeling that at any moment it would crumble away in his hand. Captain Mouso seemed oblivious of any danger, and the mate was flat on his face, bottle falling from his hand as his body slid nearer and nearer to the side.

"Better help him," Hawkmoon said.

Captain Mouso laughed. "He's all right—he's got a drunkard's luck."

But now the mate's body was against the starboard rail, his head and one shoulder already through. Hawkmoon leaped down the companionway to grab the man and haul him back to safety as the ship heaved again, this time in the other direction, and salt waves washed the deck.

Hawkmoon looked down at the man he had rescued. The mate lay on his back, eyes closed, lips moving in the words of the song he'd been singing.

Hawkmoon laughed, shaking his head, calling up to the skipper, "You're right—he has a drunkard's luck." Then, as he turned his head to port, he thought he saw something in the water. The light was fading fast, but he was sure he had seen a vessel not too far away.

"Captain—do you see anything yonder?" he yelled, going to the rail and peering into the mass of heaving water.

"Looks like a raft of some kind," Mouso called back.

Hawkmoon was soon able to see the thing more closely as a wave swept it nearer. It was a raft, with three men clinging to it.

"Shipwrecked by the look of 'em," Mouso called casually. "Poor bastards." He shrugged his shoulders. "Ah, well, not our affairs . . ."

"Captain, we must save them," Hawkmoon said.

"We'll never do it in this light. Besides, we're wasting time. I'm carrying no cargo save yourself on this trip and have to be in Simferopol on time to pick up my cargo before someone else does."

"We must save them," Hawkmoon said firmly. "Oladahn—a rope."

The Bulgar beast-man found a coil of rope in the wheelhouse and came hurrying down with it. The raft was still in sight, its burden flat on their faces, clinging to it for dear life. Sometimes it vanished in a great trough of water, reappearing after several seconds, a fair distance from the boat. The gap between them was widening at every moment, and Hawkmoon knew that there was very little time before the raft would be too far away for them to reach it. Lashing one end of the rope to the rail and looping the other about his waist, he stripped off cloak and sword and dived into the foaming ocean.

At once, Hawkmoon realized the danger he was in. The great waves were almost impossible to swim against, and there was every chance of his being dashed against the side of the ship, stunned, and drowned. But he struggled on through the water, fighting to keep it out of his mouth and eyes as he searched about for the raft.

There it was! And now its occupants had seen the ship and were standing up, waving and shouting. They had not seen Hawkmoon swimming toward them.

As he swam, Hawkmoon caught glimpses of the men from time to time, but he could not distinguish them clearly. Two now seemed to be struggling, while the third seemed to be sitting upright watching them.

"Hold on!" Hawkmoon called above the crash of the sea and the moan of the wind. Exerting all his strength, he swam even harder and was soon nearly upon the raft as it was tossed on a wild chaos of black and white water.

Then Hawkmoon caught the edge of the raft and saw that indeed two of the men were fighting in earnest. He saw, too, that they wore the snouted masks of the Order of the Boar. The men were warriors of Granbretan.

For an instant Hawkmoon debated leaving them to their fate. But if he did that, he reasoned, he would be no better than they. He must do his best to save them, then decide what to do with them.

He called up to the fighting pair, but they did not seem to hear him. They grunted and cursed in their struggle, and Hawkmoon wondered if they had not been demented by their ordeal.

Hawkmoon tried to heave himself onto the raft, but the water and the rope around his body dragged him down. He saw the seated figure look up and sign to him almost casually.

"Help me," Hawkmoon gasped, "or I'll not be able to help you."

The figure rose and swayed across the raft until his way was blocked by the fighting men. With a shrug he seized their necks, paused for an instant until the raft dipped in the water, then pushed them into the sea.

"Hawkmoon, my dear friend!" came a voice from within the boar mask. "How happy I am to see you. There—I've helped you. I've lightened our load . . ."

Hawkmoon made a grab at one of the drowning men who struggled with his companion. In the heavy masks and armor, they were bound to be dragged down in seconds. But he could not reach them. He watched in fascination as, with seeming gradualness, the masks sank below the waves.

He glared up at the survivor, who was leaning down to offer him a hand. "You have murdered your friends, D'Averc! I've a good mind to let you go down with them."

"Friends? My dear Hawkmoon, they were no such thing. Servants, aye, but not friends." D'Averc braced himself as another wave tossed the raft, nearly forcing Hawkmoon to lose his grasp. "They were loyal enough —but dreadfully boring. And they made fools of themselves. I cannot tolerate that. Come along let me help you aboard my little vessel. It is not much, but . . ."

Hawkmoon allowed D'Averc to drag him onto the raft, then turned and waved toward the ship, just visible through the darkness. He felt the rope tighten as Oladahn began to haul on it.

"It was fortunate that you were passing," D'Averc said coolly as slowly they were drawn toward the ship. "I had thought myself as good as drowned and all my glorious promise barely fulfilled—and then who should come by in his splendid ship but the noble Duke of Köln. Fate flings us together once again, Duke."

"Aye, but I'll readily fling you away again as you flung your friends, if you do not hold your tongue and help me with this rope," growled Hawkmoon.

The raft plunged through the sea and at last bumped against *Smiling Girl's* half-rotten side. A rope ladder snaked down, and Hawkmoon began to climb, finally hauling himself with relief over the rail, gasping for breath.

When Oladahn saw the next man's head emerge over the side, he cursed and made to draw his sword, but Hawkmoon stopped him. "He's our prisoner, and we might as well keep him alive, for he could be a useful bargaining counter if we are in trouble later."

"How sensible!" D'Averc exclaimed admiringly, then began coughing. "Forgive me—my ordeal has desperately weakened me, I fear. A change of clothes, some hot grog, a good night's rest, and I'll be myself again."

"You'll be lucky if we let you rot in the bilges," Hawkmoon said. "Take him below to our cabin, Oladahn."

Huddled in the tiny cabin that was dimly lit by a small lantern hanging from the roof, Hawkmoon and Oladahn watched D'Averc strip himself of his mask, armour and sodden undergarments.

"How did you come to be on the raft, D'Averc?" Hawkmoon asked as the Frenchman fussily dried himself. Even he was slightly nonplussed by the man's apparent coolness. He admired the quality and even wondered if he did not actually like D'Averc in some strange way. Perhaps it was D'Averc's honesty in admitting his ambition, his unwillingness to justify his actions, even if, as recently, they involved casual murder.

"A long story, my dear friend. The three of us—

Ecardo, Peter, and I—left the men to deal with that blind monster you released upon us and managed to reach the safety of the hills. A little later the ornithopter we had sent to collect you arrived and began to circle, evidently puzzled by the disappearance of an entire city—as we were, I must admit; you must explain that to me later. Well, we signaled to the pilot, and he came down. We had already realized the somewhat difficult position we found ourselves in. . . ." D'Averc paused. "Is there any food to be had?"

"The skipper has ordered some supper from the galley," Oladahn said. "Continue."

"We were three men without horses in a rather barren part of the world. As well, we had failed to keep you when we had captured you, and as far as we knew, the pilot was the only living man left who knew that we had done that . . . ."

"You killed the pilot?" Hawkmoon said.

"Just so. It was necessary. Then we boarded his machine with the intention of reaching the nearest base."

"What happened?" Hawkmoon asked. "Did you know how to control the ornithopter?"

D'Averc smiled. "You have guessed correctly. My knowledge is limited. We managed to gain the air, but then the wretched thing would not be steered. Before we knew it, it was carrying us off to the Runestaff knows where. I feared for my safety, I must admit. The monster behaved increasingly erratically, until at last it began to fall. I managed to guide it so that it landed on a soft riverbank, and we were barely hurt. Ecardo and Peter had become hysterical, quarreling among themselves, becoming unbearable in their manners and most hard to control. However, we somehow managed to build a raft with the intention of floating down the river until we came to a town. . . ."

"That same raft?" Hawkmoon asked.

"The same, aye."

"Then how did you come to be at sea?"

"Tides, my good friend," D'Averc said with an airy

wave of his hand. "Currents. I had not realized we were so close to an estuary. We were swept along at a most appalling rate, carried far beyond land. On that raft—that damnable raft—we spent the next several days, with Peter and Ecardo whining at one another, blaming one another for their predicament when they should have blamed me. Oh, I cannot tell you what an ordeal it was, Duke Dorian."

"You deserved worse," Hawkmoon said.

There came a knock on the cabin door. Oladahn answered it and admitted a scruffy cabin boy carrying a tray on which were three bowls containing some kind of gray stew.

Hawkmoon accepted the tray and handed D'Averc a bowl and a spoon. For a moment D'Averc hesitated; then he took a mouthful. He seemed to eat with great control. He finished the dish and replaced the empty bowl on the tray. "Delicious," he said. "Quite perfect, for ship's cooking."

Hawkmoon, who had been nauseated by the mess, handed D'Averc his own bowl, and Oladahn too, proffered his.

"I thank you," said D'Averc. "I believe in moderation. Enough is as good as a feast."

Hawkmoon smiled slightly, once again admiring the Frenchman's coolness. Evidently the food had tasted as foul to him as it had to them, but his hunger had been so great that he had eaten the stuff anyway, and with panache.

Now D'Averc stretched, his rippling muscles belying his claim to invalidism. "Ah," he yawned. "If you will forgive me, gentlemen, I will sleep now. I have had a trying and tiring few days."

"Take my bed," Hawkmoon said, indicating his cramped bunk. He did not mention that earlier he had noticed what had seemed to be a whole catalogue of lice nesting in it. "I'll see if the skipper has a hammock."

"I am grateful," D'Averc said, and there seemed to

be a surprising seriousness about his tone that made Hawkmoon wheel away from the door.

"For what?"

D'Averc began to cough ostentatiously, then looked up and said in his old, mocking tone, "Why, my dear Duke, for saving my life, of course."

In the morning the storm had died down, and though the sea was still rough it was much calmer than the previous day.

Hawkmoon met D'Averc on deck. The man was dressed in coat and britches of green velvet but was without his armor. He bowed when he saw Hawkmoon.

"You slept well?" asked Hawkmoon.

"Excellently." D'Averc's eyes were full of humour, and Hawkmoon guessed that he had been bitten a good many times.

"Tonight we should make port," Hawkmoon told him. "You will be my prisoner—my hostage, if you like."

"Hostage? Do you think the Dark Empire cares if I live or die once I have lost my usefulness?"

"We shall see," said Hawkmoon, fingering the jewel in his skull. "If you attempt to escape, I shall certainly kill you—as coolly as you killed your men."

D'Averc coughed into the handkerchief he carried. "I owe you my life," he said. "So it is yours to take if you would."

Hawkmoon frowned. D'Averc was far too devious for him to understand properly. He was beginning to regret his decision. The Frenchman might prove more of a liability than he had bargained for.

Oladahn came hurrying along the deck. "Duke Dorian," he panted, pointing forward. "A sail—and it's heading directly toward us."

"We're in little danger," Hawkmoon smiled. "We're no prize for a pirate."

But moments later Hawkmoon noticed signs of panic

among the crew, and as the captain stumbled past, he caught his arm. "Captain Mouso—what is it?"

"Danger sir," rasped the skipper. "Great danger. Did you not read the sail?"

Hawkmoon peered toward the horizon and saw that the ship carried a single black sail. On it was painted an emblem of some kind, but he could not make out what it was. "Surely they'll not trouble us," he said. "Why should they risk a fight for a tub like this—and you said yourself we're carrying no cargo."

"They care not what we carry or don't carry, sir. They attack anything on the ocean on sight. They're like killer sharks, Duke Dorian—their pleasure is not in taking treasure, but in destruction!"

"Who are they? Not a Granbretanian ship by the look of it," D'Averc said.

"Even one of those would probably not bother to attack us," stuttered Captain Mouso. "No—that is a ship crewed by those belonging to the Cult of the Mad God. They are from Muskovia and in recent months have begun to terrorize these waters."

"They definitely seem to have the intention of attacking," D'Averc said lightly. "With your permission, Duke Dorian, I'll go below and don my sword and armor."

"I'll get my weapons, too," Oladahn said. "I'll bring your sword for you."

"No point in fighting!" It was the mate, gesticulating with his bottle. "Best throw ourselves in the sea now."

"Aye," Captain Mouso nodded, looking after D'Averc and Oladahn as they went to fetch their weapons. "He's right. We'll be outnumbered, and they'll tear us to pieces. If we're captured, they'll torture us for days."

Hawkmoon started to say something to the captain, then turned as he heard a splash. The mate had gone— as good as his word. Hawkmoon rushed to the side but could see nothing.

"Don't bother to help him—follow him," the skipper said, "for he's the wisest of us all."

The ship was bearing down on them now, its black sail painted with a pair of great red wings, and in the center of them was a huge, bestial face, howling as if in the throes of maniacal laughter. Crowding the decks were scores of naked men wearing nothing but sword belts and metal-studded collars. Drifting across the water came a weird sound that Hawkmoon could not at first make out. Then he glanced at the sail again and knew what it was.

It was the sound of wild, insane laughter; as if the damned of hell were moved to merriment.

"The Mad God's ship," said Captain Mouso, his eyes beginning to fill with tears. "Now we die."

Chapter Seven

THE RING ON THE FINGER

HAWKMOON, OLADAHN, AND D'AVERC stood shoulder to shoulder by the port rail of the ship as the weird vessel sped closer.

The members of the crew had clustered around their captain, keeping as far as possible from the attackers.

Looking at the rolling eyes and foaming mouths of the madmen in the ship, Hawkmoon decided that their chances were all but hopeless. Grappling irons snaked out from the Mad God's ship and bit into the soft wood of *Smiling Girl*'s rail. Instantly the three men backed at the ropes, severing most of them.

Hawkmoon yelled to the captain, "Get your men aloft—try to turn the ship." But the frightened sailors did not move. "You'll be safer in the rigging!" Hawkmoon shouted. They began to stir but still did nothing.

Hawkmoon was forced to return his attention to the attacking ship and was horrified to see it looming over them, its insane crew clustering against the rail, some already beginning to climb over, ready to leap onto *Smiling Girl*'s deck, cutlasses drawn. Their laughter filled the air, and bloodlust shone on their twisted faces.

The first came flying down on Hawkmoon, naked body gleaming, sword raised. Hawkmoon's own blade rose to skewer the man as he fell; another twist of the sword and the corpse dropped down through the narrow gap between the ships, into the sea. Within moments the air was full of naked warriors swinging on ropes, jumping wildly, clambering hand over hand across the grappling lines. The three men stopped the first wave, hacking about them until everything seemed blood-red, but gradually they were forced away from the rail as the madmen swarmed onto the deck, fighting without skill but with a chilling disregard for their own lives.

Hawkmoon became separated from his comrades, did not know if they lived or had been killed. The prancing warriors flung themselves at him, but he clutched his battle blade in both hands and swung it about him in a great arc, this way and that, surrounding himself with a blur of bright steel. He was covered in blood from head to foot; only his eyes gleamed, blue and steady, from the visor of his helmet.

And all the while the Mad God's men laughed— laughed even as their heads were chopped from their necks, their limbs from their bodies.

Hawkmoon knew that eventually weariness would overcome him. Already the sword felt heavy in his hands and his knees shook. His back against a bulkhead, he hacked and stabbed at the seemingly ceaseless wave of giggling madmen whose swords sought to slash the life from him.

Here a man was decapitated, there another dismembered, but every blow drained more energy from Hawkmoon.

Then, as he blocked two swords that struck at him

at once, his legs buckled and he went down to one knee. The laughter grew louder, triumphant, as the Mad God's men moved in for the kill.

He hacked upward desperately, gripping the wrist of one of his attackers and wrenching the sword away from him so that now he had two blades. Using the madman's sword to thrust and his own to swing, he managed to regain his footing, kicked out at another man, and scrambled away, to rush up the companionway to the bridge. At the top of the companionway he turned to fight again, this time with an increased advantage over the howling madmen who crowded up the steps toward him. He saw now that both D'Averc and Oladahn were in the rigging, managing to keep their attackers at bay. He glanced toward the Mad God's ship. It was still held fast by grappling ropes, but it was deserted. Its entire crew was on board the *Smiling Girl*. Hawkmoon at once had an idea.

He wheeled about, running from the warriors, leaped to the rail, and grabbed a rope that trailed from the crosstrees. Then he flung himself into space.

He prayed that the rope would be long enough as he hurtled through the air, then let go, diving, it appeared, over the side of the ship. His grasping hands just managed to catch the rail of the enemy ship as he fell. He hauled himself onto the deck and began slashing at the grappling ropes, yelling "Oladahn—D'Averc! Quickly —follow me!"

From the rigging of the other ship the two men saw him and began climbing higher, to walk precariously along the main mast's yardarm while the men of the Mad God swarmed behind them.

The Mad God's ship was already beginning to slide away, the gap between it and *Smiling Girl* widening rapidly.

D'Averc jumped first, diving for the black-sailed ship's rigging and clutching a rope one-handed, to swing for an instant, threatening to drop to his death.

Oladahn followed him, cutting loose a rope and swinging across the gap, to slide down the rope and land on the deck, where he fell spread-eagled on his face.

Several of the insane warriors tried to follow, and a number actually managed to reach the deck of their own ship. Still laughing, they came at Hawkmoon in a bunch, doubtless judging Oladahn dead.

Hawkmoon was hard put to defend himself. A blade slashed his arm, another caught his face below the visor. Then suddenly, from above, a body dropped into the center of the naked warriors and began hewing around him, almost as much maniac as they.

It was D'Averc in his boar-headed armor, streaming with the blood of those he had slain. And now, at the back of their attackers came Oladahn, evidently only winded by his fall, yelling a wild mountain battle cry.

Soon every one of the madmen who had managed to reach the ship was dead. The others were leaping from the deck of *Smiling Girl* into the water, still laughing weirdly, trying to swim after the ship.

Looking back at *Smiling Girl,* Hawkmoon saw that miraculously most of her crew had apparently survived —at the last minute they had climbed to the safety of the mizzen mast.

D'Averc raced forward and took the wheel of the Mad God's ship, cutting the lashings and steering from the vainly swimming men.

"Well," breathed Oladahn, sheathing his sword and inspecting his cuts, "we seem to have escaped lightly —and with a better ship."

"With luck we'll beat *Smiling Girl* into port," Hawkmoon grinned. "I hope she's still bound for Crimia, for she has all our possessions on board."

Skillfully, D'Averc was turning the ship about toward the north. The single sail bulged as it caught the wind and the boat left the swimming madmen behind. Even as they drowned, they continued to laugh.

After they had helped D'Averc relash the wheel so that the ship continued roughly on course, they began to explore the ship. It was crammed with treasure evidently pillaged from a score of ships, but also there were all kinds of useless things—broken weapons and ships' instruments, bundles of clothing—and here and there a rotting corpse or a dismembered body, all piled together in the holds.

The three men decided to get rid of the corpses first, wrapping them in cloaks or bundling up the various limbs in rags and tossing them overboard. It was disgusting work and took a long time, for some of the remains were hidden under mounds of other things.

Suddenly Oladahn paused as he worked, his eyes fixed on a severed human hand that had become mummified in some way. Reluctantly, he picked it up, inspecting a ring on the little finger. He glanced at Hawkmoon.

"Duke Dorian. . . ."

"What is it? Do not bother to save the ring. Just get rid of the thing."

"No—it is the ring itself. Look—it has a peculiar design. . . ."

Impatiently Hawkmoon crossed the dimly lit hold and peered at the thing, gasping as he recognized it. "No! It cannot be!"

The ring was Yisselda's. It was the ring Count Brass had placed on her finger to mark her betrothal to Dorian Hawkmoon.

Numbed with horror, Hawkmoon took the mummified hand, a look of incomprehension on his face.

"What is it?" Oladahn whispered. "What is it that so disturbs you?"

"It is hers. It is Yisselda's."

"But how could she have come to be sailing this ocean so many hundreds of miles from the Kamarg? It is not possible, Duke Dorian."

"The ring is hers." Hawkmoon gazed at the hand, inspecting it eagerly as realization struck him. "But—the hand is not. See, the ring barely fits the little finger. Count Brass placed it on the middle finger, and even then it was a loose fit. This is the hand of some thief." He wrenched the precious ring from the finger and threw the hand down. "Someone who was in the Kamarg, perhaps, and stole the ring. . . ." He shook his head. "It's unlikely. But what is the explanation?"

"Perhaps she journeyed this way—seeking you, maybe," Oladahn suggested.

"She'd be foolish if she did. But it is just possible. However, if that's the case, where is Yisselda now?"

Oladahn was about to speak, when there came a low, terrifying chuckling sound from above. They looked up at the entrance to the hold.

A mad, grinning face looked down at them. Somehow one of the insane warriors had managed to catch the ship. Now he prepared to leap down on them.

Hawkmoon just managed to draw his sword as the madman attacked, sword slashing. Metal hit metal.

Oladahn drew his own blade, and D'Averc came rushing up, but Hawkmoon shouted, "Take him alive! We must take him alive!"

As Hawkmoon engaged the madman, D'Averc and Oladahn resheathed their swords and fell on the warrior's back, grasping his arms. Twice he shook them off, but then he went down kicking as they wound length after length of rope around him. And then he lay still, chuckling up at them, his eyes unseeing, his mouth foam-flecked.

"What use is he alive?" D'Averc asked with polite curiosity. "Why not cut his throat and have done with him?"

"This," Hawkmoon said, "is a ring I found just now." He held it up. "It belongs to Yisselda, Count Brass's daughter. I want to know how these men got it."

"Strange," D'Averc said frowning. "I believe the girl is in the Kamarg, nursing her father."

"So Count Brass is wounded?"

D'Averc smiled. "Aye. But the Kamarg holds against

us. I'd sought to disturb you, Duke Dorian. I do not know how badly Count Brass is hurt, but he still lives. And that wise man of his, Bowgentle, helps him command his troops. The last I heard, it was stalemate between the Dark Empire and the Kamarg."

"And you heard nothing of Yisselda? Nothing of her leaving the Kamarg?"

"No," said D'Averc, frowning. "But I seem to remember . . . Ah, yes—a man serving in Count Brass's army. I believe he was approached and persuaded to try to kidnap the girl, but the attempt was unsuccessful."

"How do you know?"

"Juan Zhinaga—the man—disappeared. Presumably Count Brass discovered his perfidy and slew him."

"I find it hard to believe that Zhinaga should be a traitor. I knew the man slightly—a captain of cavalry, he was."

"Captured by us in the second battle against the Kamarg." D'Averc smiled. "I believe he was a German, and we had some of his family in our safekeeping. . . ."

"You blackmailed him!"

"He was blackmailed, though do not give me the credit. I merely heard of the plan during a conference in Londra between the various commanders who had been summoned by King Huon to inform him of developments in the campaigns we are waging in Europe."

Hawkmoon's brow furrowed. "But suppose Zhinaga was successful—somehow not managing to reach your people with Yisselda, being stopped on the way by the Mad God's men. . . ."

D'Averc shook his head. "They would never range as far as southern France. We should have heard of them if they had."

"Then what is the explanation?"

"Let us ask this gentleman," D'Averc suggested,

prodding at the madman, whose chuckles had died down now so that they were almost inaudible.

"Let us hope we can get sense from him," Oladahn said dubiously.

"Would pain do the trick, do you think?" D'Averc asked.

"I doubt it," Hawkmoon said. "They know no fear. We must try another method." He looked in disgust at the madman. "We'll leave him for a while and hope he calms a little."

They went up on deck, closing the hatch cover. The sun was beginning to set, and the coastline of Crimia was now in sight—black crags sharp against the purple sky. The water was calm and dappled with the fading sunlight, and the wind blew steadily northward.

"I'd best correct our course," D'Averc suggested. "We seem to be sailing a little too far to the north." He moved along the deck to unbind the wheel and spin it several points south.

Hawkmoon nodded absently, watching D'Averc, his great mask flung back from his head, expertly controlling the course of the ship.

"We'll have to anchor offshore tonight," Oladahn said, "and sail in in the morning."

Hawkmoon did not reply. His head was full of unanswered questions. The exertions of the past twenty-four hours had brought him close to exhaustion, and the fear in his mind threatened to drive him to a madness fully as dreadful as that of the man in the hold.

Later that night, by the light of lamps suspended from the ceiling, they studied the sleeping face of the man they had captured. The lamps swung as the ship rocked at anchor, casting shifting shadows on the sides of the hold and over the great piles of booty heaped everywhere. A rat chittered, but the men ignored the sound. They had all slept a little and felt more relaxed.

Hawkmoon knelt down beside the bound man and touched his face. Instantly the eyes opened, staring around dully, no longer mad. They even seemed a little puzzled.

"What is your name?" Hawkmoon asked.

"Coryanthum of Kerch—who are you? Where am I?"

"You should know," Oladahn said. "On board your own ship. Do you not remember? You and your fellows attacked our vessel. There was a fight. We escaped from you, and you swam after us and tried to kill us."

"I remember setting sail," Coryanthum said, his voice bewildered, "but nothing else." Then he tried to struggle up. "Why am I bound?"

"Because you are dangerous," D'Averc said lightly. "You are mad."

Coryanthum laughed, a purely natural laugh. "I mad? Nonsense!"

The three looked at one another, puzzled. It was true that the man seemed to have no hint of madness about him now.

Understanding began to dawn on Hawkmoon's face. "What is the very last thing you remember?"

"The captain addressing us."

"What did he say?"

"That we were to take part in a ceremony—drinking a special drink. . . . Nothing much more." Coryanthum frowned. "We drank the drink. . . ."

"Describe your sail," Hawkmoon said.

"Our sail? Why?"

"Is there anything special about it?"

"Not that I remember. It's canvas—a dark blue. That's all."

"You are a merchant seaman?" Hawkmoon asked.

"Aye."

"And this is your first voyage on this ship?"

"Aye."

"When did you sign on?"

Coryanthum looked impatient. "Last night, my friend—on the Day of the Horse by Kerch reckoning."

"And in universal reckoning?"

The sailor wrinkled his brow. "Oh—the eleventh of the third month."

"Three months ago," said D'Averc.

"Eh?" Coryanthum peered through the gloom at the Frenchman. "Three months? What d'you mean?"

"You were drugged," Hawkmoon explained. "Drugged and then used to commit the foulest acts of piracy ever heard of. Do you know anything of the Cult of the Mad God?"

"A little. I heard that it is situated somewhere in Ukrania and that its adherents have been venturing out lately—even onto the high seas."

"Did you know that your sail now bears the sign of the Mad God? That a few hours ago, you raved and giggled in mad bloodlust? Look at your body. . . ." Hawkmoon bent down to cut the bonds. "Feel your neck."

Coryanthum of Kerch stood up slowly, wondering at his own nakedness, his fingers going slowly to his neck and touching the collar there. "I—I don't understand. Is this a trick?"

"An evil trick, and one we did not commit," Oladahn said. "You were drugged until you went insane, then ordered to kill and collect all the loot you could. Doubtless your 'merchant captain' was the only man who knew what would happen to you, and it's almost certain he's not aboard now. Do you remember anything? Any instructions about where you should go?"

"None."

"Without doubt the captain meant to rejoin the ship later and guide it to whatever port he uses," D'Averc said. "Maybe there is a ship in regular contact with the others, if they are all full of such fools as this one."

"There must be a large supply of the drug somewhere aboard," Oladahn said. "Doubtless they fed off it regularly. It was only because we bound this fellow that he did not get the chance to replenish himself."

"How do you feel?" Hawkmoon asked the sailor.

"Weak—drained of all life and feeling."

"Understandable," said Oladahn. "It's sure that the drug kills you in the end. A monstrous plan! Take innocent men, feed them a drug that turns them mad and ultimately destroys them, use them to murder and loot, then collect the proceeds. I've heard of nothing like it before. I'd thought the Cult of the Mad God to be comprised of honest fanatics, but it seems a cooler intelligence controls it."

"On the seas, at any rate," Hawkmoon said. "However, I'd like to find the man responsible for all this. He alone may know where Yisselda is."

"First, I'd suggest we take up the sail," D'Averc said. "We'll drift into the harbor on the tide. Our reception would not be pleasant if they saw our sail. Also, we can make use of this treasure. Why, we are rich men!"

"You are still my prisoner, D'Averc," Hawkmoon reminded him. "But it is true we could dispose of some of the treasure, since the poor souls who owned it are all dead now, and give the rest into the safekeeping of some honest man, to compensate those who have lost relatives and fortunes at the hands of the mad sailors."

"Then what?" asked Oladahn.

"Then we set sail again—and wait for this ship's master to seek her out."

"Can we be sure he will? What if he hears of our visit to Simferopol?" Oladahn asked.

Hawkmoon smiled grimly. "Then doubtless he will still wish to seek us out."

Chapter Eight

MAD GOD'S MAN

AND SO THE loot was sold in Simferopol, some of it used to provision the craft and buy new equipment and horses, and the rest given into the safekeeping of a merchant whom all recommended as the most honest in the whole of Crimia. Not much behind the captured ship, *Smiling Girl* limped in, and Hawkmoon hastily bought the captain's silence regarding the nature of the black-sailed ship. He recovered his possessions, including the saddlebag containing Rinal's gift, and, with Oladahn and D'Averc, reboarded the ship, sailing on the evening tide. They left Coryanthum with the merchant to recover.

For more than a week the black ship drifted, usually becalmed, for the wind had dropped to almost nothing. By Hawkmoon's reckoning they were drifting close to the channel that separated the Black Sea from the Azov Sea, near to Kerch, where Coryanthum had been recruited.

D'Averc lounged in a hammock he had hung for himself amidships, occasionally coughing theatrically and remarking on his boredom. Oladahn sat often in the crowsnest, scanning the sea, while Hawkmoon paced the decks, beginning to wonder if his plan had had any substance to it other than his need to know what had become of Yisselda. He was even beginning to doubt that the ring had been hers, deciding that perhaps several such rings had been made in the Kamarg over the years.

Then, one morning, a sail appeared on the horizon, coming from the northwest. Oladahn saw it first and called to Hawkmoon to come on deck. Hawkmoon rushed up and peered ahead. It might be the ship they awaited.

"Get below," he called. "Everybody get below."

Oladahn scrambled down the rigging, while D'Averc, suddenly active, swung out of his hammock and strolled to the ladder that led belowdecks. They met in the darkness of the central hold and waited. . . .

An hour seemed to pass before they heard timber bump against timber and knew that the other ship had drawn alongside. It might still be an innocent vessel curious about a ship drifting apparently unmanned.

Not much later Hawkmoon heard the sound of booted feet on the deck above; a slow, measured tread that went the length of the whole deck and back again. Then there was silence as the man above entered a cabin or climbed to the bridge.

Tension grew as the sound of the footsteps came again, this time walking directly toward the central hold.

Hawkmoon saw a silhouette above, peering down into the darkness where they crouched. The figure paused, then began to descend the ladder. As he did so, Hawkmoon crept forward.

When the newcomer had reached the bottom, Hawkmoon sprang, his arm encircling the man's throat. He was a giant, more than six and a half feet tall, with a huge black bushy beard and plaited hair, wearing a brass breastplate over his shirt of black silk. He growled in surprise and swung around, carrying Hawkmoon with him. The giant was incredibly strong. His huge fingers went up to Hawkmoon's arm and began to prise it loose.

"Quick—help me hold him," Hawkmoon cried, and his friends rushed forward to fling themselves on the giant and bear him down.

D'Averc drew his sword. Wearing his boar mask and the metal finery of Granbretan, he looked dangerous and terrible as he delicately placed the tip of his sword against the giant's throat.

"Your name?" D'Averc demanded, his voice booming in his helmet.

"Captain Shagarov. Where is my crew?"

The black-bearded giant glared up at them, unabashed by his capture. "Where is my crew?"

"You mean the madmen you sent akilling?" Oladahn said. "They are drowned, all but one, and he told us of your evil treachery."

"Fools!" Shagarov cursed. "You are three men. Did

you think to trap me—when I have a shipful of fighters aboard my other ship?"

"We have disposed of one shipload, as you'll note," D'Averc told him with a chuckle. "Now that we are used to the work, doubtless we can dispose of another."

For a moment fear crept into Shagarov's eyes; then his expression hardened. "I do not believe you. Those who sailed this ship lived only to kill. How could you . . . ?"

"Well, we did," D'Averc said. He turned his great, helmeted head toward Hawkmoon. "Shall we go on deck and put the rest of our plan into operation?"

"A moment." Hawkmoon bent close to Shagarov. "I want to question him. Shagarov—did you men capture a girl at any time?"

"They had orders not to kill any girl but to bring them to me."

"Why?"

"I know not—I was ordered to send girls to him— and girls I sent him." Shagarov laughed. "You'll not keep me for long, you know. You'll all three be dead within an hour. The men will get suspicious."

"Why didn't you bring any of them aboard with you? Perhaps because they are not madmen—because even they might be disgusted by what they found?"

Shagarov shrugged. "They'll come when I yell."

"Possibly," said D'Averc. "Rise, please."

"These girls," Hawkmoon continued. "Where did you send them—and to whom?"

"Inland, of course, to my master—the Mad God."

"So you do serve the Mad God—you are not deceiving people into believing these acts of piracy are committed by his followers."

"Aye—I serve him, though I'm no cult member. His agents pay me well to raid the seas and send the booty to him."

"Why this way?"

Shagarov sneered. "The cult has no sailing men. So one of them conceived this plan to raise money—

though I know not the purpose for the loot—and approached me." He rose to his feet, towering over them. "Come—let's go up. It will amuse me to see what you do."

D'Averc nodded to the other two, who went back into the shadows and produced long, unlit brands, one for each of them. D'Averc prodded at Shagorov to follow Oladahn up the companionway.

Slowly they climbed to the deck, to emerge at last in the sunlight and see a big, handsome three-master anchored beside them.

The men on board the other ship understood at once what had happened and made to move forward, but Hawkmoon dug his sword into Shagarov's ribs and called, "Do not move, or we will kill your captain."

"Kill me—and they kill you," Shagarov rumbled. "Who gains?"

"Silence," said Hawkmoon. "Oladahn, light the brands."

Oladahn applied flint and tinder to the first brand. It flared into life. He lit the others off it and handed one each to his companions.

"Now," Hawkmoon said. "This ship is covered in oil. Once we touch our brands to it, the whole vessel goes up in flames—and most likely your ship too. So we advise you to make no move toward rescuing your captain."

"So we all burn," Shagarov said. "You're as mad as the ones you slew."

Hawkmoon shook his head. "Oladahn, ready the skiff."

Oladahn went aft to the furthermost hatch, swinging a derrick over it, hauling back the hatch cover, and then disappearing below, taking the cable with him.

Hawkmoon saw the men on the other ship begin to stir and he moved the brand menacingly. The heat from it turned his face dark red, and the flames reflected fiercely in his eyes.

Now Oladahn re-emerged and began to work the

specially geared winch with one hand while holding his brand with the other. Slowly something began to appear in the hatch, something that barely cleared the wide opening.

Shagarov grunted in surprise as he saw that it was a large skiff in which three horses were harnessed, looking frightened and bewildered as they were hauled to the deck and then swung out over the sea.

Oladahn stopped his work and leaned back on the winch, panting and sweating, but made sure to keep the brand well away from the timber of the deck.

Shagarov scowled. "An elaborate plan—but you are still only three men. What do you intend to do now?"

"Hang you," said Hawkmoon. "Before the eyes of your crew. Two things motivated me in laying this trap for you. One—I needed information. Two—I determined to give you justice."

"Whose *justice?*" Shagarov bellowed, his eyes full of fear. "Why involve yourselves in the affairs of others? We did no harm to you. Whose justice?"

"Hawkmoon's justice," said the pale-faced Duke of Köln. Caught by the rays of the sun, the sinister black jewel in his forehead seemed to glow with life.

"Men!" Shagarov screamed across the water. "Men —rescue me. Attack them."

D'Averc called back, "If you move toward him, we kill him and set the ship ablaze. You gain nothing. If you'd save your own lives and your ship, you'll shove off and leave us. Our quarrel is with Shagarov."

As they had expected, the crew commanded by the pirate did not feel any great loyalty to him and, when their own skins were threatened, felt no great compulsion to come to his help. Yet they did not cast off the grappling irons but waited to see what the three men would do next.

Now Hawkmoon swung up into the crosstrees. He carried a rope with a noose already knotted. When he reached the top, he flung the rope over the arm so that it hung over the water, tied it firmly, and came down again to the deck.

Now there was silence as Shagarov slowly realized that he could expect no assistance from his men.

Up aft, the skiff with its burden of horses and provisions swung slightly in the still air, the davits creaking. The brands flared and puttered in the hands of the three companions.

Shagarov shouted and tried to break away, but three swords stopped him, points at his throat, chest, and belly.

"You cannot . . ." Shagarov's voice trailed off as he saw the determination on the faces of the three.

Oladahn reached out and hooked the dangling rope with his sword, bringing it to the rail. D'Averc pushed Shagarov forward, Hawkmoon took the noose and widened it to place it over Shagarov's head. Then, as the noose settled around his neck, Shagarov bellowed and struck out at Oladahn, who was perched on the rail. With a shout of surprise, the little man toppled and plunged into the water. Hawkmoon gasped and rushed to see how Oladahn fared. Shagarov turned on D'Averc, knocking the brand from his hand, but D'Averc stepped back and flourished his sword under Shagarov's nose.

The pirate captain spat in his face and leaped to the rail, kicked out at Hawkmoon, who tried to stop him; then the captain leaped into space.

The noose tightened, the yardarm bent, then straightened, and Captain Shagarov's body danced wildly up and down. His neck snapped, and he died.

D'Averc dashed for the fallen brand, but it had already ignited the oil-soaked deck. He began stamping on the flames.

Hawkmoon rushed to fling a rope to Oladahn, who, dripping, climbed up the side of the ship, looking none the worse for his swim.

Now the crew of the other vessel began to mutter

and move about, and Hawkmoon wondered why they did not cast off.

"Shove off!" he called, as Oladahn regained the deck. "You cannot save your captain now—and you're in danger from the fire!"

But they did not move.

"The fire, you fools!" Oladahn pointed to where D'Averc was retreating from the flames, which were now leaping high, touching the mast and superstructure.

D'Averc laughed. "Let's to our little boat."

Hawkmoon flung his own brand after D'Averc's and turned. "But why don't they get away?"

"The treasure," said D'Averc as they lowered the skiff to the water, the frightened horses snorting as they sniffed the fire. "They think the treasure's still aboard."

As soon as the skiff was afloat, they clambered down the lines into the boat and cut themselves adrift. Now the black ship was a mass of flame and oily smoke. Outlined against the fire, the body of Shagarov swung, twisting this way and that as if trying to avoid the hellish heat.

They let loose the skiff's sail, and the breeze filled it, bearing them away from the blazing vessel. Now, beyond it, they could see the pirate's ship, a sail smoldering as sparks from the other ship caught it. Some of the crew were busy putting it out while others were reluctantly casting off the grappling lines. But now it was touch and go whether the fire would spread through their own ship.

Soon the skiff was too far away for them to see whether the pirate ship was safe or not, and in the other direction, land was in sight. The land of Crimia and beyond it, Ukrania.

And somewhere in Ukrania they would find the Mad God, his followers, and possibly Yisselda. . . .

BOOK TWO

Now, WHILE DORIAN Hawkmoon and his companions sailed for Crimia's mountainous shore, the armies of the Dark Empire pressed in upon the little land of the Kamarg, ordered by Huon, the King-Emperor, to spare no life, energy, and inspiration in the effort to crush and utterly destroy those upstarts who dared resist Granbretan. Across the Silver Bridge that spanned thirty miles of sea came the hordes of the Dark Empire, pigs and wolves, vultures and dogs, mantises and frogs, with armor of strange design and weapons of bright metal. And in his throne globe, curled foetus-like in the fluid that preserved his immortality, King Huon burned with hatred for Hawkmoon, Count Brass and the rest who, somehow, he could not contrive to manipulate as he manipulated the rest of the world. It was as if some counterforce aided them—perhaps manipulated them as he could not—and this thought the King-Emperor refused to tolerate. . . .

But much depended on those few beyond the power of King Huon's influence, those few free souls—Hawkmoon, Oladahn, perhaps D'Averc, the mysterious Warrior in Jet and Gold, Yisselda, Count Brass, and a handful of others. For on these the Runestaff relied to work its own pattern of destiny. . . .

—*The High History of the Runestaff*

Chapter One
THE WAITING WARRIOR

As THEY NEARED the bleak crags marking the shore, Hawkmoon glanced curiously at D'Averc, who had flung back his boar-masked helm and was staring out to sea, a slight smile on his lips. D'Averc seemed to sense Hawkmoon's attention and glanced at him.

"You are puzzled, Duke Dorian," he said. "Are you not a little pleased by the outcome of our plan?"

"Aye." Hawkmoon nodded. "But I wonder about you, D'Averc. You joined in this venture spontaneously; yet there is no gain in it for you. I am sure you were not greatly interested in bringing Shagarov his deserts, and you certainly do not share my desperation in wanting to know Yisselda's fate. Also, you have not to my knowledge made any attempt to escape."

D'Averc's smile broadened a little. "Why should I? You do not threaten my life. In fact, you saved my life. At this point, my fortunes seem linked closer to yours than the Dark Empire's."

"But your loyalty is not to me and my cause."

"My loyalty, my dear Duke, as I have already explained, is to the cause most likely to further my own ambition. I must admit I've changed my views about the hopelessness of your own—you seem endowed with such monstrous good luck I am sometimes even inclined to think you might win against the Dark Empire.

If that seems possible, I might well join you, and with great enthusiasm."

"You do not bide your time, perhaps, hoping to reverse our roles again and capture me for your masters?"

"No denial would convince you," D'Averc smiled, "so I will not offer you one."

The enigmatic answer set Hawkmoon to frowning again.

As if to change the topic of conversation, D'Averc suddenly doubled up with a coughing fit and lay down, panting, in the boat.

Oladahn called out now from the prow. "Duke Dorian! Look—on the beach!"

Hawkmoon peered ahead. Now, under the looming cliffs, he could make out a narrow strip of shingle. A horseman could be seen on the beach, motionless, looking towards them as if he awaited them with some particular message.

The keel of the skiff scraped the shingle of the beach, and Hawkmoon recognized the horseman who waited in the shadow of the cliff.

Hawkmoon sprang from the boat and approached him. He was clad from head to foot in plate armor, his helmeted head bowed as if in brooding thought.

"Did you know I would be here?" Hawkmoon asked.

"It seemed that you might beach in this particular place," replied the Warrior in Jet and Gold. "So I waited."

"I see." Hawkmoon looked up at him, uncertain what to do or say next. "I see. . . ."

D'Averc and Oladahn came crunching up the beach towards them.

"You know this gentleman?" D'Averc asked lightly.

"An old acquaintance," Hawkmoon said.

"You are Sir Huillam d'Averc," said the Warrior in Jet and Gold sonorously. "I see you still wear the garb of Granbretan."

"It suits my taste," D'Averc replied. "I did not hear you introduce yourself."

The Warrior in Jet and Gold ignored D'Averc, raising a heavy, gauntleted hand to point at Hawkmoon. "This is the one I must speak with. You seek your betrothed, Yisselda, Duke Dorian, and you quest for the Mad God."

"Is Yisselda a prisoner of the Mad God?"

"In a manner of speaking, yes. But you must seek the Mad God for another reason."

"Yisselda lives? Does she live?" Hawkmoon said insistently.

"She lives."

"The Warrior in Jet and Gold shifted in his saddle. "But you must destroy the Mad God before she can be yours again. You must destroy the Mad God and rip the Red Amulet from his throat—for the Red Amulet is rightfully yours. Two things the Mad God has stolen, and both those things are yours—the girl and the amulet."

"Yisselda is mine, certainly—but I know of no amulet. I have never owned one."

"This is the Red Amulet, and it is yours. The Mad God has no right to wear it, and thus it turned him mad."

Hawkmoon smiled. "If that is the Red Amulet's property, then the Mad God is welcome to it."

"This is not a matter for humour, Duke Dorian. The Red Amulet has turned the Mad God mad because he stole it from a servant of the Runestaff. But if the Runestaff's servant wears the Red Amulet, then he is able to derive great power transmitted from the Runestaff through the amulet. Only a wrongful wearer is turned mad—only the rightful wearer may regain it once another wears it. Therefore, I could not take it from him, nor could any man save Dorian Hawkmoon von Köln, servant of the Runestaff."

"Again you call me servant of the Runestaff; yet I know of no duties I must perform, do not even know if this is all a fabric of imaginings and you are some madman yourself."

"Think what you wish. However, there is no doubt, is there, that you seek the Mad God—that you desire nothing greater than to find him?"

"To find Yisselda, his prisoner . . ."

"If you like. Well, then, I need not convince you of your mission."

Hawkmoon frowned. "There has been a strange series of coincidences since I embarked on the journey from Hamadan. Barely credible."

"There are no coincidences where the Runestaff is concerned. Sometimes the pattern is noticed, sometimes it is not." The Warrior in Jet and Gold turned in his saddle and pointed to a winding path cut into the cliff side. "We can ascend there. Camp and rest above. In the morning we shall begin the journey to the Mad God's castle."

"You know where it lies?" Hawkmoon asked eagerly, forgetting his other doubts.

"Aye."

Then another thought occurred to Hawkmoon. "You did not . . . did not *engineer* Yisselda's capture? To force me to seek the Mad God?"

"Yisselda was captured by a traitor in her father's army—Juan Zhinaga, who planned to take her to Granbretan. But he was diverted on the way by warriors of the Dark Empire who wished to claim the credit for kidnapping her. While they fought, Yisselda escaped and fled, joining, at length, a refugee caravan through Italia, managing to get passage, sometime later, on a ship sailing the Adriatic Sea, bound, she was told, ultimately for Provence. But the ship was a slaver, running girls to Arabia, and in the Gulf of Sidra was attacked by a pirate vessel from Karpathos."

"It is a hard story to believe. What then?"

"Then the Karpathians decided to ransom her, not knowing that the Kamarg was under siege but learning only later of the impossibility of getting money from that quarter. They decided to take her to Istanbul to sell her, but arrived to find the harbor full of Dark Empire ships. Fearing these, they sailed on into the Black Sea, where the ship was attacked by the one you have just burned. . . ."

"I know the rest. That hand I found must have belonged to a pirate who stole Yisselda's ring. But it is a wild tale, Warrior, and barely has the sound of truth. Coincidence . . ."

"I told you—there are no coincidences where the Runestaff is involved. Sometimes the pattern seems simpler than at other times."

Hawkmoon sighed. "She is unharmed?"

"Relatively."

"What do you mean?"

"Wait until you come to the Mad God's castle."

Hawkmoon tried to question the Warrior in Jet and Gold further, but the enigmatic man remained entirely silent. He sat on his horse, apparently deep in thought, while Hawkmoon went to help D'Averc and Oladahn get the nervous horses out of the boat and unload the rest of the provisions they had brought. Hawkmoon found his battered saddlebag still safe and marveled at his being able to hold on to it through all their adventures.

When they were ready, the Warrior in Jet and Gold silently turned his horse and led the way to the steep cliff path, beginning to climb it without pause.

The three companions, however, were forced to dismount and follow after him at a much slower pace. Several times both men and horses stumbled and seemed about to fall, loose stones dropping away beneath their feet, to hurtle to the shingle that was now far below them. But at last they gained the top of the cliff and looked over a hilly plain that seemed to stretch away forever.

The Warrior in Jet and Gold pointed to the west. "In the morning, we go that way, to the Throbbing Bridge. Beyond that lies Ukrania, and the Mad God's castle lies many days' journey into the interior. Be wary, for Dark Empire troops roam thereabouts."

He watched as they made camp. D'Averc looked up at him. "Won't you join us in our meal, sir?" he said almost sardonically.

But the great, helmeted head remained bowed, and both warrior and horse stood stock still, like a statue, remaining thus all night, as if watching over them—or possibly watching them to make sure they did not leave on their own.

Hawkmoon lay in his tent looking out at the silhouette of the Warrior in Jet and Gold, wondering if the creature were in any way human, wondering if his interest in Hawkmoon was ultimately friendly or malign. He sighed. He wanted only to find Yisselda, save her, and take her back to the Kamarg, there to satisfy himself that the province still stood against the Dark Empire. But his life was complicated by this strange mystery of the Runestaff and some destiny he must work out that fitted with the Runestaff's "scheme." Yet the Runestaff was a thing, not an intelligence. Or was it an intelligence? It was the greatest power one could call upon when oath making. It was believed to control all human history. Why, then, he wondered, should it need "servants" if, in effect, all men served it?

But perhaps not all men did. Perhaps there emerged forces from time to time—like the Dark Empire—that were opposed to the Runestaff's scheme for human destiny. Then, perhaps, the Runestaff needed servants.

Hawkmoon became confused. His was not these days the head for profundity of that sort, nor speculative philosophy. Not much later he fell asleep.

Chapter Two

THE MAD GOD'S CASTLE

FOR TWO DAYS they rode until they came to the Throbbing Bridge, which spanned a stretch of sea running between two high cliffs some miles apart.

The Throbbing Bridge was an astonishing sight, for it did not seem made of any kind of solid substance at all, but of a vast number of criss-crossed beams of coloured light that seemed somehow to have been plaited. Gold and shining blue were there, and bright, gleaming scarlet and green and pulsing yellow. All the bridge throbbed like some living organ, and below, the sea foamed on sharp rocks.

"What is it?" Hawkmoon asked the Warrior in Jet and Gold. "Surely no natural thing?"

"An ancient artifact," said the warrior, "wrought by a forgotten science and a forgotten race who sprang up sometime between the fall of the Death Rain and the rise of the Princedoms. Who they were and how they were brought into being and died, we do not know."

"Surely you know," D'Averc said cheerfully. "You disappoint me. I had judged you omniscient."

The Warrior in Jet and Gold made no reply. The light from the Throbbing Bridge was reflected on their skins and armor, staining them a variety of hues. The horses began to prance and became difficult to control as they directed them closer to the great bridge of light.

Hawkmoon's horse bucked and snorted, and he tightened its reins, forcing it forward. At last its hooves touched the throbbing light of the bridge and it became calmer as it realized that the bridge would actually bear its weight.

The Warrior in Jet and Gold was already crossing the bridge, his whole body seeming to be ablaze with a multicolored aura, and Hawkmoon, too, saw the strange light creep around the body of his horse and then immerse him in a weird radiance. Looking back he saw D'Averc and Oladahn shining like beings from another star as they moved slowly over the bridge of throbbing light.

Below, faintly seen through the criss-cross of beams, were the gray sea and the foam-encircled rocks. And in Hawkmoon's ears there grew a humming sound that was musical and pleasant, yet seemed to set his whole frame vibrating gently in time with the bridge itself.

At length they were across, and Hawkmoon felt fresh, as if he had had several days' rest. He mentioned this to the Warrior in Jet and Gold who said, "Aye, that's another property of the Throbbing Bridge, I'm told."

Then they rode on, with only land now between them and the Mad God's lair.

On the third day of their journey it had begun to rain, a fine drizzle that chilled them and lowered their spirits. Their horses plodded across the vast, sodden Ukranian plains, and it seemed that there was no end to the grey world.

On the sixth day of their journey, the Warrior in Jet and Gold raised his head and brought his horse to a halt, signaling for the other three to stop. He appeared to be listening.

Soon Hawkmoon heard the sound too—the drumming of horses' hooves. Then, breasting a slight rise to their left, came some score of riders in sheep-skin hats and cloaks, long spears and sabres on their backs.

They seemed in a panic, and not noticing the four onlookers, they rode past at fantastic speed, lashing the rumps of their steeds until blood flew in the air.

"What is it?" Hawkmoon called. "What do you flee from?"

One of the riders turned in his saddle, not lessening

his speed. "Dark Empire army!" he called, and dashed on.

Hawkmoon frowned. "Should we continue in this direction?" he asked the warrior. "Or should we find another route?"

"No route is safe," replied the Warrior in Jet and Gold. "We might just as well take this one."

Within half an hour they saw smoke in the distance. It was thick, oily smoke that crept close to the ground, and it stank. Hawkmoon knew what the smoke signified but said nothing until, later, they came to the town that was burning and saw, piled in the square, a huge pyramid of corpses, every one naked—men, women, children, and animals heaped indiscriminately upon one another and burning.

It was this pyre of flesh that gave off the evil-smelling smoke, and there was only one race Hawkmoon knew of who would indulge in such an act as this. The riders had been right. Dark Empire soldiers were nearby. There were signs that a whole battalion of troops had taken the town and razed it.

They skirted around the town, for there was nothing they could do, and in even more sobre spirits continued on their journey, wary now for any sign of Granbretanian troops.

Oladahn, who had not witnessed so many of the Dark Empire's atrocities, was the one most visibly moved by the sight they had witnessed.

"Surely," he said, "ordinary mortals could not . . . could not . . ."

"They do not regard themselves as ordinary mortals," D'Averc said. "They regard themselves as demigods and their rulers as gods."

"It excuses their every immoral action in their eyes," Hawkmoon said. "And besides, they love to wreak destruction, spread terror, torture and kill. Just as in some beasts, like the wolverine, the urge to kill is stronger even than the urge to live, so it is with those of the Dark Empire. The island has bred a race of madmen whose every thought and action is alien to those not born on Granbretan."

The depressing drizzle continued to fall as they left the town and its blazing pyramid behind.

"It is not far now to the Mad God's castle," said the Warrior in Jet and Gold.

By the next morning they had come to a wide, shallow valley and a small lake on which a gray mist moved. Beyond the lake they saw a black, gloomy shape, a building of rough-hewn stone that lay on the far side of the water.

About midway between the castle and themselves, they could see a collection of rotting hovels clustered on the shore and a few boats drawn up nearby. Nets had been hung out to dry, but there was no sign of the fishers who used them.

The whole day was dark, cold, and oppressive, and there was an ominous atmosphere about lake, village, and castle. The three men followed reluctantly behind the Warrior in Jet and Gold as he made his way around the shore toward the castle.

"What of this Mad God's cult?" Oladahn whispered. "How many men does he command? And are they as ferocious as those we fought on the ship? Does the warrior underestimate their strength or overestimate our prowess?"

Hawkmoon shrugged, his only thought for Yisselda. He scanned the great black castle, wondering where she was imprisoned.

As they came to the fisherfolk's village they saw why it was so silent. Every last villager had been slain, hacked down by swords or axes. Some of the blades were still buried in skulls of men and women alike.

"The Dark Empire!" said Hawkmoon.

But the Warrior in Jet and Gold shook his head. "Not their work. Not their weapons. Not their way."

"Then . . . what?" murmured Oladahn, shivering. "The cult?"

The warrior did not answer. Instead, he reined in his horse and dismounted, walking heavily toward the nearest corpse. The others dismounted also, looking warily about them. The mist from the lake curled around them like some malign force that sought to trap them.

The warrior pointed at the corpse. "All these were members of the cult. Some served by fishing to provide the castle with its food. Others lived in the castle itself. Some of these are from the castle."

"They have been fighting among themselves?" D'Averc suggested.

"In a sense, perhaps," replied the warrior.

"How do you mean—?" Hawkmoon began, but then whirled as a chilling shriek came from behind the hovels. All drew their weapons, standing in a hollow circle, prepared for an attack from any side.

But when the attack did come, the nature of the attackers caused Hawkmoon to lower his sword momentarily in astonishment.

They came running between the houses, swords and axes raised. They were dressed in breastplates and kilts of leather, and a ferocious light burned in their eyes. Their lips were drawn back in bestial snarls. Their white teeth gleamed, and foam flecked their mouths.

But this was not what astonished Hawkmoon and his companions. It was their sex that caught them by surprise, for all the maniacally shrieking warriors rushing at them were women of incredible beauty.

As he slowly recovered his defensive stance, Hawkmoon desperately sought among the faces for that of Yisselda and was relieved that he did not find it.

"So this is why the Mad God demanded women be sent to him," D'Averc gasped. "But why?"

"He is a perverse god I understand," said the Warrior in Jet and Gold as he brought up his blade to meet the attack of the first warrior woman.

Though he defended himself desperately against the blades of the mad-faced women, Hawkmoon found it impossible to counterattack. They left many openings for his sword, and he could have slain several, but every time he had the opportunity to strike, he held back. And it seemed to be the same with his companions. In a moment's respite he glanced around him, and an idea came.

"Retreat slowly," he said to his friends. "Follow me. I've a plan to make this our victory—and a bloodless one."

Gradually the four fell back until they were stopped by the poles on which the stout nets of the fishermen had been hung out to dry. Hawkmoon stepped around the first and seized one end of the net, still battling. Oladahn guessed his scheme and grabbed the other end; then Hawkmoon cried, "Now!" and they flung the thing out over the heads of the women.

The net settled over most of them, entangling them. But some slashed free and came on.

Now D'Averc and the Warrior in Jet and Gold understood Hawkmoon's intention, and they, too, flung a net to trap those who had escaped. Hawkmoon and Oladahn hurled a third net over the group they had originally ensnared. Eventually the women were completely trapped in the folds of several strong nets, and the companions were able to approach them gingerly, grabbing at their weapons and gradually disarming them.

Hawkmoon panted as he raised a sword and flung it into the lake. "Perhaps the Mad God is not so insane. Train women to fight and they'll always have a certain momentary advantage over male soldiers. Doubtless this was part of some larger scheme. . . ."

"You mean his raising money by piracy was to finance a conquering army of women?" Oladahn said, joining him in hurling weapons into the water while the struggles of the women subsided behind them.

"It seems likely," D'Averc agreed, watching them work. "But why did the women kill the others?"

"That we may find out when we reach the castle,"

said the Warrior in Jet and Gold. "We—" He broke off as part of one of the nets burst and a howling warrior woman came rushing at them, fingers outstretched like claws. D'Averc seized her, encircling her waist with his arms as she kicked and shrieked. Oladahn stepped up, reversed his sword, and struck her on the base of the skull with the pommel.

"Much as it offends my sense of chivalry," D'Averc said, lowering the prone girl to the ground, "I think that you have presented the best scheme for dealing with these pretty murderesses, Oladahn," and he crossed to the nets, to begin languidly and systematically knocking out the struggling women fighters. "At least," he said, "we have not killed them—and they have not killed us. An excellent equilibrium."

"I wonder if they are the only ones," Hawkmoon said broodingly.

"You are thinking of Yisselda?" Oladahn asked.

"Aye, I'm thinking of Yisselda. Come." Hawkmoon swung into his saddle. "Let's to the Mad God's castle." He began to gallop rapidly along the beach toward the great black pile. The others were slower in following, straggling behind him. First came Oladahn, then the Warrior in Jet and Gold, and finally Huillam d'Averc at a leisurely canter, looking for all the world like a carefree youth out for a morning ride.

The castle came closer, and Hawkmoon slowed his mad dash, hauling on his horse's reins and bringing it to a skidding halt as they reached the drawbridge.

Within the castle all was quiet. A little mist curled about its towers. The drawbridge was down, and on it lay the corpses of the guards.

Somewhere, from the tops of one of the highest towers, a raven squawked and flapped away over the water of the lake.

No sun shone through those gray clouds. It was as if no sun had ever shone here, as if no sun ever would shine. It was as if they had left the world for some

limbo where hopelessness and death prevailed through-
out eternity.

The dark entrance to the castle courtyard gaped at
Hawkmoon.

The mist formed grotesque shapes, and there was an
oppressive silence everywhere. Hawkmoon took a deep
breath of the chill, damp air, drew his blade, kicked at
the flanks of his horse, and charged across the drawbridge, leaping the corpses, to enter the Mad God's lair.

Chapter Three

HAWKMOON'S DILEMMA

THE GREAT COURTYARD of the castle was clogged
with bodies. Some were of the warrior women, but
most were of men wearing the collar of the Mad God.
Dried blood caked the cobbles not occupied by
corpses in grotesque attitudes.

Hawkmoon's horse snorted in fear as the stench of
decaying flesh filled its nostrils, but he urged it on,
dreading that he would see Yisselda's face among the
dead.

He dismounted, turning over stiff bodies of women,
peering at them closely, but none was Yisselda.

The Warrior in Jet and Gold entered the courtyard,
Oladahn and D'Averc behind him. "She is not here,"
said the warrior. "She is alive—within."

Hawkmoon's bleak face rose. His hand trembled as it
took the bridle of his horse. "Has—has he done ought
to her, Warrior?"

"That you must see for yourself, Sir Champion."
The Warrior in Jet and Gold pointed at the castle's main
doorway. "Through there lies the court of the Mad
God. A short passage leads to the main hall, and there
he sits awaiting you. . . ."

"He knows of me?"

"He knows that one day the Red Amulet's rightful wearer must arrive to claim what is his. . . ."

"I care nothing for the amulet, only for Yisselda. Where is she, Warrior?"

"Within. She is within. Go claim both your rights— your woman and your amulet. Both are important to the Runestaff's scheme."

Hawkmoon turned and ran for the doorway, disappearing into the darkness of the castle.

The interior of the castle was incredibly chill. Cold water dripped from the roof of the passage, and moss grew on the walls. Blade in hand, Hawkmoon crept along it, half-expecting an attack.

But none came. He reached a large wooden door, stretching twenty feet above his head, and paused.

From behind the door came a strange rumbling sound, a deep-voiced murmuring that seemed to fill the hall beyond. Cautiously Hawkmoon pushed against the door, and it yielded. He put his head through the gap and peered in upon a bizarre scene.

The hall was of strangely distorted proportions. In some parts the ceilings were very low, in others they soared upward for fifty feet. There were no windows, and the light came from brands stuck at random in the walls.

In the center of the hall, on a floor on which one or two corpses lay as they had been cut down earlier, was a great chair of black wood, studded with inlaid plaques of brass. In front of this, swinging from a part of the ceiling that was relatively low, was a large cage, such as would be used for a tame bird, save that this was much bigger. In it, Hawkmoon saw huddled a human figure.

Otherwise, the weird hall was deserted, and Hawkmoon entered, creeping across the floor toward the cage.

It was from this, he realized, that the distressed muttering sound was coming; yet it seemed impossible, for the noise was so great. Hawkmoon decided that it was because the sound was amplified by the peculiar acoustics of the hall.

He reached the cage and could see the huddled figure only dimly, for the light was poor.

"Who are you?" Hawkmoon asked. "A prisoner of the Mad God?"

The moaning ceased, and the figure stirred. From it then came a deep, echoing melancholy voice. "Aye— you could say so. The unhappiest prisoner of all."

Now Hawkmoon could make out the creature better. It had a long, stringy neck, and its body was tall and very thin. Its head was covered in long, straggling gray hair that was matted with filth, and it had a pointed beard, also filthy, that jutted from its chin for about a foot. Its nose was large and aquiline, and its deepset eyes held the light of a melancholy madness.

"Can I save you?" Hawkmoon said. "Can I prise apart the bars?"

The figure shrugged. "The door of the cage is not locked. Bars are not my prison. I have been trapped within my groaning skull. Ah, pity me."

"Who are you?"

"I was once known as Stalnikov, of the great family of Stalnikov."

"And the Mad God usurped you?"

"Aye. Usurped me. Aye, exactly." The prisoner in the unlocked cage turned his huge, sad head to stare at Hawkmoon. "Who are you?"

"I am Dorian Hawkmoon, Duke of Köln."

"A German?"

"Köln was once part of the country called Germania."

"I have a fear of Germans." Stalnikov slid back in the cage, farther away from Hawkmoon.

"You need not fear me."

"No?" Stalnikov chuckled, and the mad sound filled the hall. "No?" He reached into his jerkin and pulled something forth that was attached to a throng about his neck. The thing glowed within a deep red light, like a huge ruby, illuminated from within, and Hawkmoon saw that it bore the sign of the Runestaff. "No? Then you are not the German who has come to steal my power?"

Hawkmoon gasped. "The Red Amulet! How did you obtain it?"

"Why," said Stalnikov, rising and grinning horribly at Hawkmoon, "I obtained it thirty years ago from the corpse of a warrior my retainers set upon and slew as he rode this way." He fondled the amulet, and its light struck Hawkmoon in the eyes so that he could barely see. *"This* is the Mad God. *This* is the source of my madness and my power. *This* is what imprisons me!"

"You are the Mad God! Where is my Yisselda?"

"Yisselda? The girl? The new girl with the blonde hair and the white, soft skin? Why do you ask?"

"She is mine."

"You do not want the amulet?"

"I want Yisselda."

The Mad God laughed, and his laughter filled the hall and reverberated through every cranny of the distorted place. "Then you shall have her, German!"

He clapped his clawlike hands, his whole body moving like a loose-limbed puppet's, the cage swinging wildly. "Yisselda, my girl! Yisselda, come forth to serve your master!"

From the depths of one part of the hall where the ceiling almost touched the floor, a girl emerged. Hawkmoon saw her outlined but could not be fully sure it was Yisselda. He sheathed his sword and moved forward. Yes . . . the movements, the stance—they were Yisselda's.

A smile of relief began to form on his lips as he stretched out his arms to embrace her.

Then there came a wild animal shriek, and the girl rushed at him, metal-taloned fingers reaching for his eyes, face distorted with blood-lust, every part of her body enclosed in a garment studded with outward-jutting spikes.

"Kill him, pretty Yisselda," chuckled the Mad God. "Kill him, my flower, and we shall reward you with his offal."

Hawkmoon put up his hands to fend off the claws, and the back of one of them was slashed badly. He backed away hastily. "Yisselda, no—it is your betrothed, Dorian. . . ."

But the mad eyes showed no sign of recognition, and the mouth slavered as the girl slashed again with the talons of metal. Hawkmoon leaped away, pleading with his eyes that she might recognize him. "Yisselda . . ."

The Mad God chuckled, grasping the bars of his cage and looking on eagerly. "Slay him, my chicken. Rip his throat."

Hawkmoon was almost weeping now as he leaped this way and that to avoid Yisselda's gleaming talons.

He called to Stalnikov. "What power is it she obeys that conquers her love for me?"

"She obeys the power of the Mad God, as I obey it," Stalnikov answered. "The Red Amulet makes all its slaves!"

"Only in the hands of an evil creature . . ." Hawkmoon flung himself aside as Yisselda's talons ripped at him. He scrambled up and darted toward the cage.

"It turns all who wear it evil," Stalnikov replied, chuckling as Yisselda's claws ripped at Hawkmoon's sleeve. "All . . ."

"All but a servant of the Runestaff!"

The voice came from the entrance to the hall, and it belonged to the Warrior in Jet and Gold. It was sonorous and grave.

"Help me," said Hawkmoon.

"I cannot," said the Warrior in Jet and Gold, standing motionless, his huge blade point down on the floor before him, his gauntleted hands resting on the pommel.

Now Hawkmoon stumbled and felt Yisselda's claws digging into his back. He lifted his hands to grab her wrists and yelled in pain as the spikes sank into his palms, but he managed to free himself of the talons and fling her away and dash for the cage where the Mad God gibbered in delight.

Hawkmoon leaped for the bars, kicking at Stalnikov as he did so. The cage swung erratically and began to spin. Yisselda danced below, trying to reach him with her talons.

Stalnikov had withdrawn to the opposite side of the cage, his mad eyes now full of terror, and Hawkmoon managed to drag open the door and fling himself in, pulling it shut behind him. Outside, Yisselda howled in frustrated bloodlust, the light from the amulet turning her eyes scarlet.

Now Hawkmoon wept openly as he darted a glance at the woman he loved; then he turned his hate-filled face on the Mad God.

Stalnikov's deep voice, still mournful, reverberated through the hall. He fingered the amulet, directing its light into Hawkmoon's eyes. "Back, mortal. Obey me —obey the amulet. . . ."

Hawkmoon blinked, feeling suddenly weak. His eyes became fixed on the glowing amulet, and he paused, feeling the power of the thing engulf him.

"Now," said Stalnikov. "Now, you will deliver yourself up to your destroyer."

But Hawkmoon rallied all his determination and took a step forward. The Mad God's bearded chin dropped in astonishment. "I command you in the name of the Red Amulet . . ."

From the doorway came the sonorous voice of the Warrior in Jet and Gold. "He is the one whom the amulet cannot control. The only one. He is the rightful wearer."

Stalnikov trembled and began to edge around the cage as Hawkmoon, still weak, moved determinedly on.

"Back!" screamed the Mad God. "Leave the cage!"

Below, Yisselda's taloned fingers had grasped the bars and she was hauling her metal studded body up, her eyes still fixed murderously on Hawkmoon's throat.

"Back!" This time Stalnikov's voice lost some of its

force and confidence. He reached the door of the cage and kicked it open.

Yisselda, her white teeth bared, her beautiful face twisted in terrifying madness, had hauled herself up now so that she clung to the outside of the cage. The Mad God's back was toward her, the Red Amulet directed still into Hawkmoon's eyes.

Yisselda's claw darted out, slashing at the back of Stalnikov's head. He screamed and leaped to the floor. Now Yisselda saw Hawkmoon again and made to enter the cage.

Hawkmoon knew there was no time to try to reason with his maddened betrothed. He gathered all his strength and dived past her slashing claw, to land on the uneven flagstones of the floor and lie there for a moment, winded.

Painfully he picked himself up as Yisselda, too, leaped groundward.

The Mad God had scrambled to the great seat opposite the cage, climbing up its back to perch there, the Red Amulet dangling from his neck, casting its strange light again on Hawkmoon's face. Blood streamed down his shoulders from the wound Yisselda's clawed hands had inflicted.

Stalnikov gibbered in terror as Hawkmoon reached the seat and climbed up onto its arm. "I beg you, leave me . . . I'll do you no harm."

"You've done me much harm already," Hawkmoon said grimly, drawing his blade. "Much harm. Enough to make revenge taste very sweet, Mad God. . . ."

Stalnikov crept as high as he could. He shouted at the girl. "Yisselda—stop! Resume your former character. I command you, by the power of the Red Amulet!"

Hawkmoon turned and saw that Yisselda had paused, looking bemused. Her lips parted in horror as she stared at the things on her hands, the metal spikes that covered her body. "What has happened? What has been done to me?"

"You were hypnotized by this monster here," Hawkmoon waved his sword in the cringing Stalnikov's direction. "But I will avenge the wrongs he has done you."

"No," Stalnikov screamed. "It is not fair!"

Yisselda burst into tears.

Stalnikov looked this way and that. "Where are my minions—where are my warriors?"

"You made them destroy one another for your own perverted sport," Hawkmoon told him. "And those not slain, we captured."

"My army of women! I wanted beauty to conquer all Ukrania. Get me back the Stalnikov inheritance . . ."

"That inheritance is here," said Hawkmoon, raising his sword.

Stalnikov leaped from the back of the chair and began to run toward the door but swerved aside as he saw that it was blocked by the Warrior in Jet and Gold.

He scuttled into the darkness of the hall, into a cranny where he disappeared from sight.

Hawkmoon got down from the chair and turned to look at Yisselda, who lay in a heap on the floor weeping. He went to her and gently removed the blood-stained talons from her slim, soft fingers.

She looked up. "Oh, Dorian. How did you find me? Oh, my love . . ."

"Thank the Runestaff," said the voice of the Warrior in Jet and Gold.

Hawkmoon turned, laughing in relief. "You are persistent in your claims, at least, Warrior."

The Warrior in Jet and Gold said nothing but stood like a statue, faceless and tall, by the doorway.

Hawkmoon discovered the fastenings of the grim, spiked suit and began to strip it off the girl.

"Find the Mad God," said the Warrior. "Remember, the Red Amulet is yours. It will give you power."

Hawkmoon frowned. "And turn me mad, perhaps?"

"No, fool, it is yours by right."

Hawkmoon paused, impressed by the Warrior's tone.

Yisselda touched his hand. "I can do the rest," she said.

Hawkmoon hefted his sword and peered into the darkness wherein Stalnikov, the Mad God, had disappeared.

"Stalnikov!"

Somewhere in the deepest recesses of the hall a tiny spot of red light gleamed. Hawkmoon ducked his head and entered the alcove. He heard a sobbing sound. It filled his ears.

Closer and closer crept Hawkmoon to the source of the red brilliance. Greater and greater became the sound of the strange weeping. Then at last the red glow burned very bright, and by its light he saw the wearer of the amulet, standing against a wall of rough-hewn stone, a sword in his hand.

"For thirty years I have waited for you, German," Stalnikov said suddenly, his voice calming. "I knew you must come to ruin my plans, to destroy my ideals, to demolish all I have worked for. Yet I hoped to avert the threat. Perhaps I still can."

With a great scream, he raised the sword and swung it at Hawkmoon.

Hawkmoon blocked the blow easily, turned the blade so that it spun from the Mad God's grasp, brought his own sword forward so that it was presented at Stalnikov's heart.

For a moment Hawkmoon looked gravely and broodingly at the frightened madman. The light from the Red Amulet stained both their faces scarlet. Stalnikov cleared his throat as if to plead; then his shoulders sagged.

Hawkmoon drove the point of his blade into the Mad God's heart. Then he turned on his heel and left both corpse and Red Amulet where they lay.

Chapter Four

THE POWER
OF THE AMULET

HAWKMOON DREW HIS cloak about Yisselda's naked shoulders. The girl was shivering, sobbing with reaction mixed with joy at seeing Hawkmoon. Nearby stood the Warrior in Jet and Gold, still motionless.

While Hawkmoon embraced Yisselda, the warrior began to move, his huge body crossing the hall and entering the darkness where lay the body of Stalnikov, the Mad God.

"Oh, Dorian, I cannot tell you the horrors I have been through these past months. Captured by this group and that, traveling for hundreds of miles. I do not even know where this hellish place is. I have no memory of recent days, save for a faint remembrance of some nightmare where I struggled with myself against a desire to slay you. . . ."

Hawkmoon hugged her to him. "A nightmare was all it was. Come, we will leave. We will return to the Kamarg and safety. Tell me, what has become of your father and the others?"

Her eyes widened. "Did you not know? I had thought you returned there first before coming to seek me."

"I have heard nothing but rumors. How are Bowgentle, von Villach, Count Brass . . . ?"

She lowered her gaze. "Von Villach was killed by a flame-lance in a battle with Dark Empire troops on the northern borders. Count Brass . . ."

"What is it?"

"When I last saw him, my father lay on a sickbed, and even Bowgentle's healing powers seemed incapable of raising him to health. It is as if he had lost all feelings—as if he no longer wished to live. He said the

Kamarg must soon fall—he believed you dead when you did not return in the time necessary to have told him you were safe."

Hawkmoon's eyes blazed. "I must get back to the Kamarg—if only to give Count Brass the will again to live. With you gone, he can barely have sustained any kind of energy."

"If he lives at all," she said softly, not wanting to admit the possibility.

"He must live. If the Kamarg still stands, then Count Brass lives."

From the passage beyond the hall came the sound of running, booted feet. Hawkmoon pushed Yisselda behind him and again drew his great battle blade.

The door was flung open, and Oladahn stood there panting, D'Averc not far behind.

"Dark Empire warriors," Oladahn said. "More of them than we could fight. They must be exploring the castle and surrounds for survivors and booty."

D'Averc pushed past the little beast-man. "I tried to reason with them—claimed that I had the right to command them, being of greater rank than their leader, but"—he shrugged—"it seems D'Averc has no rank in the legions of Granbretan any more. The damned pilot of the ornithopter lived long enough to tell a search party of my clumsiness in letting you escape. I am as much an outlaw, now, as you. . . ."

Hawkmoon frowned. "Come in, both, and bar that great door. It should hold them if they attack."

"Is it the only exit?" D'Averc asked, appraising the door.

"I thank so," Hawkmoon said, "but we must worry about that score later."

From the shadows, the Warrior in Jet and Gold re-emerged. In one gloved hand the Red Amulet dangled from its cord. The cord was stained with blood.

The Warrior handled it gingerly, not touching the stone itself, and stretched it out toward Hawkmoon as

D'Averc and Oladahn hurried to swing the door shut and bar it.

"Here," said the Warrior in Jet and Gold. "It is yours."

Hawkmoon recoiled. "I do not want it—will not have it. It is an evil thing. It has caused many to die, others to go mad—even that poor creature Stalnikov was its victim. Keep it. Find another fool enough to wear it!"

"You must wear it," came the voice from the helm. "Only you may wear it."

"I will not!" Hawkmoon swept out his hand to point to Yisselda. "That thing drove this gentle girl to become a slavering, killing beast. All those we saw in the fisherfolk's village—all slain by the power of the Red Amulet. All those who came against us—turned insane by its power. All those who died in the courtyard—destroyed by the Red Amulet." He struck the thing from the Warrior's hand. "I will not take it. If that is what the Runestaff creates, I will have no part of it!"

"It is what men—fools like yourself—do with it, that makes it corrupt in its influence," the Warrior in Jet and Gold said, his voice still grave and impassive. "It is your duty—as the Runestaff's chosen servant—to take the gift. It will not harm you. It will bring you nothing but power."

"Power to destroy and turn men mad!"

"Power to do good—power to fight the hordes of the Dark Empire!"

Hawkmoon sneered. There came a great crash on the door, and he knew that the warriors of Granbretan had found them. "We are outnumbered," said Hawkmoon. "Will the Red Amulet give us the power to escape them when there is only one way out—through yonder door?"

"It will help you," said the Warrior in Jet and Gold, leaning down to retrieve the fallen amulet, again picking it up by its string.

The door creaked under the pressure of the blows from those on the other side.

"If the Red Amulet can do so much good," Hawkmoon said, "why do you not touch it yourself?"

"It is not mine to touch. It could do to me what it did to the miserable Stalnikov." The warrior moved forward. "Here, take it. It is why you came here."

"It is because of Yisselda I came here—to rescue her. I have done that."

"It is why she came here."

"So it was a trick to lure me . . . ?"

"No. It was part of the pattern. But you say you came to save her, and yet you refuse the means of escaping with her safely from this castle. Once those warriors break in, a score or more of fierce fighters, they will destroy you all. And Yisselda's fate might be worse than yours. . . ."

Now the door was splitting. Oladahn and D'Averc backed away, swords ready, a look of quiet desperation in their eyes.

"Another moment and they will be in here," said D'Averc. "Farewell, Oladahn—and you, too, Hawkmoon. You were less boring companions than some . . ."

Hawkmoon eyed the amulet. "I do not know . . ."

"Trust my word," said the Warrior in Jet and Gold. "I have saved you in the past. Would I have done so merely to destroy you now?"

"Destroy me, no—but this will deliver me into some evil power. How do I know you are a messenger for the Runestaff? I have only your word that I serve it and not some darker cause."

"The door is breaking down!" Oladahn yelled. "Duke Dorian, we'll need your aid! Let the Warrior escape with Yisselda if he can!"

"Quick," said the Warrior, extending the amulet again to Hawkmoon. "Take it and save the maid, at least."

For an instant, Hawkmoon hesitated; then he accepted the thing. It settled into his hand like a pet in the hand of its master—but an exceedingly powerful pet. Its red light grew in intensity until it flooded the great, grotesquely proportioned chamber. Hawkmoon felt the power surge into him. His whole body became full of a great sense of well-being. When he moved it was with great speed. His brain seemed no longer clouded by the events of the past day. He smiled and placed the blood-stained thong about his neck, bent to kiss Yisselda once and felt a delicious sensation rush through him, turned, sword ready, to face the howling horde that had by now all but demolished the great door.

Then the door fell inward, and there stood crouched the panting beasts of Granbretan, tiger masks gleaming with enameled metal and semiprecious jewels, weapons poised to butcher the pathetic-seeming little group that awaited them.

The leader stepped forward.

"So much exercise for so few. Brothers, we'll make them pay for our efforts."

And then the killing began.

Chapter Five

THE SLAUGHTER
IN THE HALL

"OH, BY THE Runestaff," murmured Hawkmoon thickly, "the power in me!"

Then he sprang forward, great battle blade howling through the air to snap the enmetaled neck of the leading warrior, slash backhanded at the man to his left and send him reeling, swing around and cut through the armor of the man to his right.

Suddenly there were blood and twisted metal everywhere. The light from the amulet spread scarlet shadows across the masked faces of the warriors as Hawkmoon led his comrades forward in an attack—the last thing the Dark Empire soldiers had expected.

But the amulet's light dazzled them, and they lifted armor-clumsy arms to shield their eyes, weapons held defensively bewildered by the speed with which Hawkmoon, Oladahn, and D'Averc moved against them. Following the other three came the Warrior in Jet and Gold, his own huge broadsword whistling in a circle of steel death, all his movements apparently effortless.

There was a clattering and a shouting from the men of Granbretan as, with Yisselda behind them at all times, the four drove them into the hall.

Hawkmoon was attacked by some six swearing axemen who tried to press in against him and stop him from wielding his deadly sword, but the young Duke of Köln kicked out at one, elbowed another aside, and brought his blade straight down into the mask-helmet of another splitting both helm and skull so that brains oozed through the fissure when he'd tugged his sword free. The sword became rapidly blunted with so much work, until at last he was using it more as an axe than anything else. He wrenched a fresh sword from the hand of one of his attackers but kept his own. With the new sword he thrust, with the old he hacked.

"Ah," whispered Hawkmoon. "The Red Amulet is worth its price." It swung at his neck, turning his sweating, vengeful face into a red demon's mask.

Now the last of the warriors tried to flee for the door, but the Warrior in Jet and Gold and D'Averc blocked them, hacking them down as they tried to burst past.

Somewhere, Hawkmoon caught a glimpse of Yisselda. Her face was buried in her hands as she refused to witness the red ruin Hawkmoon and his friends had created. "Oh, it is sweet to slay these carrion," Hawkmoon said. "Yisselda—this is our triumph!" But the girl did not look up.

In many parts of the hall the floors were heaped with the twisted corpses of the slaughtered. Hawk-

moon panted, seeking more to slay, but there were none
left. He dropped the borrowed blade, sheathed his own,
the battle lust leaving him completely. He frowned
down at the Red Amulet, raising it up to regard it more
closely, studying the simple motif of a runecarved staff.

"So," he murmured. "Your first help is in aiding me
to kill. I'm grateful, but I wonder, still, if you're not a
force more for evil than for good. . . ." The light from
the Runestaff flickered and began to fade. Hawkmoon
looked up at the Warrior in Jet and Gold. "The amulet's dulled—what means that?"

"Nothing," said the Warrior. "It draws its power
from a great distance off and cannot sustain it at all
times. It will grow bright again eventually." He paused,
cocking his head toward the passage. "I hear more
footsteps—the warriors were not the whole force."

"Then let us go to meet them," D'Averc said with a
low bow, waving Hawkmoon before him. "After you,
my friend. You seem best equipped to be first."

"No," said the Warrior. "I will go. The Amulet's
power has faded for the while. Come."

Warily they passed through the smashed door, Hawkmoon last with Yisselda. She looked up at him then,
her eyes steady. "I am glad you killed them," she said,
"though I hate to see death come so gracelessly."

"They live without grace," Hawkmoon said softly,
"and they deserve to die without grace. It is the only
way to treat those who serve the Dark Empire. Now we
must face more of them. Be brave, my love, for we
encounter our greatest danger."

Ahead, the Warrior in Jet and Gold had already
engaged the first of the fresh force of fighters and was
flinging the weight of his great metal-encased body
against them so that they stumbled back in the narrow
confines of the passage, unnerved, as much as anything, because not one of their opponents seemed hurt
by them and because some five and twenty of their
comrades appeared to have met their death within.

The Dark Empire soldiers broke out into the corpse-strewn courtyard, shouting and trying to rally themselves. All four who came against them were covered in partly dried blood and brains and made a terrifying sight as they entered the daylight.

The gray rain was still falling and the air was still chill, but it revived Hawkmoon and the others, and their recent victory had made them feel invincible. Hawkmoon, D'Averc, and Oladahn grinned like wolves at their foes—grinned with such complacency, too, that the Dark Empire warriors hesitated before attacking, though they greatly outnumbered Hawkmoon and his companions. The Warrior in Jet and Gold raised a pointing finger to the drawbridge. "Begone," he said in deep, grave tones, "or we shall destroy you as we destroyed your brothers."

Hawkmoon wondered if the warrior were bluffing or if that mysterious entity honestly believed they could beat so many without the power of the Red Amulet to aid them.

But before he could decide, another group of warriors came rushing over the drawbridge. They had retrieved weapons from the hands and bodies of corpses, and they were enraged.

The Mad God's warrior women had escaped from the nets.

"Show them the amulet," the Warrior in Jet and Gold whispered to Hawkmoon. "That is what they are used to obeying. It is that which bemused them in the first place, not the Mad God."

"But its light has faded," Hawkmoon protested.

"No matter. Show them the amulet."

Hawkmoon swept the Red Amulet from his neck and held it up before the howling women.

"Stay. In the name of the Red Amulet, I command you to attack not us—but these . . ." and he pointed at the wavering Dark Empire warriors. "Come, I will lead you!"

Hawkmoon sprang forward, his blunted sword

sweeping out to slash the foremost warrior and slay him before he realized it.

The women easily outnumbered the Dark Empire force, and they worked with a will at their destruction, so well that D'Averc called, "Let them finish—we can escape now."

Hawkmoon shrugged. "This is surely but one pack of Dark Empire hounds. There must be many more about, for it's not their way to spread too far from the mass of their brothers."

"Follow me," said the Warrior in Jet and Gold. "Time, I think, to unloose the Mad God's beasts. . . ."

Chapter Six

THE MAD GOD'S BEASTS

THE WARRIOR IN Jet and Gold led them to a section of the courtyard where a pair of great iron trap-doors had been let into the cobblestones. They were forced to drag aside corpses before they could grasp the huge brass rings and heave the doors back. The doors clanged on the stones to reveal a long stone ramp that led down into gloom.

From within came a warm smell that was at once familiar and unfamiliar to Hawkmoon and made him hesitate at the top of the ramp, for he was sure that the scent meant danger.

"Do not be afraid," said the warrior firmly. "Proceed. There lies your method of escaping this place."

Slowly Hawkmoon began to descend, the others following him.

The light coming thinly from above showed him a long room with a large object at the far end. He could not decide what it was and was about to investigate it, when the Warrior in Jet and Gold said from behind him, "Not now. First, the beasts. They are in their stalls."

Hawkmoon realized that the long room was in fact some sort of stable, with stalls on either side. From some of them came stirring sounds and animal grunts, and all at once a door shuddered as a huge bulk was flung against it.

"Not horses," said Oladahn. "Nor bullocks. To me, Duke Dorian, they have the smell of *cats*."

"Aye, that's so," Hawkmoon nodded, fingering the pommel of his sword. "Cats—that's the scent. How can cats aid our escape?"

D'Averc had taken a brand from the wall and was striking a flint to ignite his tinder. Shortly, the brand flamed, and Hawkmoon saw that the object at the far end of the stable was a vast chariot, large enough to accommodate more than their number. Its double shafts had space for four animals.

"Open the stalls," said the Warrior in Jet and Gold, "and harness the cats to the yokes."

Hawkmoon wheeled. "Harness cats to the chariot? Certainly a whim fit for a mad god—but we are sane mortals, Warrior. Besides, those cats are wild, by the sound of their movements. If we open the stalls, they're bound to fall upon us."

As if in confirmation, there came a great yowling roar from one of the stalls, and this was taken up by the other beasts until the stables echoed with the bestial din and it was impossible to make oneself heard over it.

When it had begun to subside, Hawkmoon shrugged and stepped toward the ramp. "We'll find horses above and take our chances with more familiar steeds than these."

"Have you not yet learned to trust my wisdom?" said the warrior. "Did I not speak truth about the Red Amulet and the rest?"

"I have still to test that truth fully," Hawkmoon said.

"Those mad women obeyed the power of the amulet, did they not?"

"They did," Hawkmoon agreed.

"The Mad God's beasts are trained, likewise, to obey he who is master of the Red Amulet. What would I gain, Dorian Hawkmoon, from lying to you?"

Hawkmoon shrugged. "I have grown suspicious of all since I first encountered the Dark Empire. I do not know if you have anything to gain or not. However"—he walked towards the nearest stall and laid his hands on the heavy wooden bar—"I'm tired of bickering and will test your assurances. . . ."

As he flung off the bar, the stable door was swept back from within by a giant paw. Then a head emerged, larger than an oxen's, fiercer than a tiger's; a snarling cat's head with slanting yellow eyes and long yellow fangs. As it padded out, a deep growling sound coming from its belly, its glaring eyes regarding them calculatingly, they saw that its back was lined with a row of foot-high spines of the same color and appearance as its fangs, running down to the base of its tail, which, unlike that of an ordinary cat, was tipped with barbs.

"A legend come to life," gasped D'Averc, losing his detached manner for a moment. "One of the mutant war jaguars of Asiacommunista. An old bestiary I saw pictured them, said that if they had existed at all then it was a thousand years ago, that because they were the products of some perverted biological experiment they could not breed. . . ."

"So they cannot," said the Warrior in Jet and Gold, "but their lifespan is all but infinite."

The huge head now swung toward Hawkmoon, and the barbed tail swished back and forth, the eyes fixing on the amulet at Hawkmoon's throat.

"Tell it to lie down," said the Warrior.

"Lie down!" commanded Hawkmoon, and almost at once the beast settled to the floor, its mouth closing, its eyes losing some of their fierceness.

Hawkmoon smiled. "I apologize, Warrior. Very well, let's loose the other three. Oladahn, D'Averc . . ."

His friends went forward to take out the bars of the remaining stalls, and Hawkmoon put his arm around Yisselda's shoulders.

"That chariot," he said, "will bear us home, my love." Then he remembered something. "Warrior, my saddle bags—still on my horse unless those dogs have stolen them!"

"Wait here," said the Warrior, turning and beginning to ascend the ramp. "I will look."

"I will look myself," Hawkmoon said. "I know the—"

"No," said the Warrior. "I will go."

Hawkmoon felt a vague suspicion. "Why?"

"Only you, with the amulet, have the power of controlling the Mad God's beasts. If you were not here, they could turn on the others and destroy them."

Reluctantly, Hawkmoon stepped back and watched the Warrior in Jet and Gold move with heavy purposefulness to the top of the ramp and disappear.

Out of their stalls now prowled three more horned cats, similar to the first. Oladahn cleared his throat nervously. "Best remind them that it is you they obey," he said to Hawkmoon.

"Lie down!" Hawkmoon commanded, and slowly the beasts did as he commanded. He went up to the nearest and laid a hand on its thick neck, feeling the wiry, bristling fur, the hard muscle beneath it. The beasts were the height of horses but considerably bulkier and infinitely more deadly. They had not been bred to pull carriages, that was plain, but to kill in battle.

"Move that chariot up," he said, "and let's harness these creatures."

D'Averc and Oladahn dragged the chariot forward. It was of black brass and green gold and smelled of antiquity. Only the leather of the yokes was relatively new. They slipped the harness over the heads and shoulders of the beasts, and the mutant jaguars hardly moved, save for flattening their ears occasionally when the men tightened the straps too rapidly.

When all was ready, Hawkmoon signed to Yisselda to enter the chariot. "We must wait for the warrior to return," he said. "Then we may set off."

"Where is he?" D'Averc asked.

"Gone to find my gear," Hawkmoon explained.

D'Averc shrugged and lowered his great helm over his face. "It is taking him long enough. I for one will be glad when we leave this place behind. It stinks of death and evil."

Oladahn pointed upward, at the same time drawing his sword. "Is that what you smelled, D'Averc?"

At the top of the ramp stood six or seven more Dark Empire warriors of the Order of the Weasel, their long-snouted masks seeming to tremble in anticipation of killing the men below.

"Into the chariot, quick," Hawkmoon ordered as the weasels descended.

In the front of the chariot was a raised block on which the driver could stand, and beside it, in a rack once used for javelins, a long-handled whip. Hawkmoon sprang onto the block, seized the whip, and cracked it over the heads of the beasts. "Up, beauties! Up!" The cats climbed to their feet. "And now—forward!"

The chariot jumped forward with a great lurch as the powerful animals dragged it up the ramp. The weasel-masked warriors screamed as the gigantic horned cats raced toward them. Some leaped from the ramp, but most were too late and went down screaming, crushed by clawed feet and iron-rimmed wheels.

Out into the gray daylight the bizarre chariot broke, scattering more weasel warriors come to investigate the open trapdoors.

"Where is the Warrior?" Hawkmoon cried above the din of howling men. "Where are my saddlebags?"

But the Warrior in Jet and Gold was nowhere to be

seen, and neither could they locate Hawkmoon's horse.

Now Dark Empire swordsmen hurled themselves against the chariot, and Hawkmoon lashed out at them with his whip while behind him Oladahn and D'Averc held them back with their own blades.

"Drive through the gate!" D'Averc cried. "Hurry— at any moment they'll overwhelm us!"

"Where is the Warrior?" Hawkmoon looked wildly about him.

"Doubtless he awaits us outside!" D'Averc shouted desperately. "Drive, Duke Dorian, or we're doomed!"

Suddenly Hawkmoon saw his horse over the heads of the milling warriors. It had been stripped of its saddlebags, and he had no way of knowing who had taken them.

In panic he shouted again, "Where is the Warrior in Jet and Gold? I must find him. The contents of those saddlebags could mean life or death for the Kamarg!"

Oladahn gripped his shoulder and said urgently, "And if you do not drive us from this place it means our deaths—and maybe worse for Yisselda!"

Hawkmoon was nearly out of his mind with indecision, but then, as Oladahn's words at last entered his consciousness, he gave a great yell and whipped up the beasts, sending them springing through the gate and across the drawbridge, to gallop along the lakeside with what seemed like all the hordes of Granbretan behind them.

Moving far more rapidly than horses could move, the Mad God's beasts dragged the bouncing chariot over the ground and away from the dark castle and the mist-covered lake, away from the village of hovels and the place of corpses, into the foothills beyond the lake, down a muddy road that led between gloomy cliffs, and onto the wide plains again. There the road petered out and the ground became soft, but the mutant jaguars had no effort in crossing it.

"If I have a complaint," remarked D'Averc, as he clung for dear life to the side of the chariot and was bounced about horribly, "it is that we are moving a trifle too rapidly. . . ."

Oladahn tried to grin through gritted teeth. He was crouched in the bottom of the vehicle, holding Yisselda and trying to protect her from the worst of the bumps.

Hawkmoon made no response. He clenched the reins tight in his hands and did not reduce the speed of their flight. His face was pale and his eyes blazed with anger, for he was sure he had been duped by the man who claimed to be his chief ally against the Dark Empire— duped by the apparently incorruptible Warrior in Jet and Gold.

Chapter Seven

ENCOUNTER IN A TAVERN

"HAWKMOON, STOP, FOR the Runestaff's sake! Stop, man! Are you possessed!" D'Averc, more troubled than anyone had ever seen him, tugged at Hawkmoon's sleeve as the man lashed at the panting beasts. The chariot had been moving for hours now, had splashed across two rivers without stopping, and was now tearing through a forest as night fell. At any moment it might strike a tree and kill them all. Even the powerful horned cats were tiring, but Hawkmoon mercilessly lashed them on.

"Hawkmoon! You are mad!"

"I am betrayed!" answered Hawkmoon. "Betrayed! I had the salvation of the Kamarg in those saddlebags, and the Warrior in Jet and Gold stole them. He tricked me. Gave me a trinket with limited powers in exchange for a machine with powers that were unlimited for my purposes! On, beasts, on!"

"Dorian, listen to him. You will kill us all!" Yisselda spoke tearfully. "You will kill yourself—and then how will you aid Count Brass and the Kamarg?"

The chariot leaped into the air and came down with a crash. No normal vehicle could have stood such a shock, and it jarred the passengers to their bones.

"Dorian! You have gone mad. The Warrior would not betray us. He has helped us. Perhaps he was overwhelmed by Dark Empire men—the saddlebags stolen from him!"

"No—I sensed some betrayal when he left the stables. He has gone—my gift from Rinal with him."

But Hawkmoon's rage and bafflement were beginning to pass, and he no longer whipped at the flanks of the straining beasts.

Gradually the pace of the chariot slowed as the tired beasts, free from the whip, gave in to their instinct to rest.

D'Averc took the reins from Hawkmoon's hands, and the young warrior did not resist, merely sank to the bottom of the chariot and buried his head in his hands.

D'Averc brought the beasts to a halt, and they fell at once to the ground, panting noisily.

Yisselda stroked Hawkmoon's hair. "Dorian—all the Kamarg needs is you to save it. I do not know what this other thing was, but I am sure we have no use for it. And you have the Red Amulet. That will be of some use, surely."

It was night now, and moonlight fell through a lattice of tree branches. D'Averc and Oladahn dismounted from the chariot, rubbing their bruised bodies, and went off to look for wood for a fire.

Hawkmoon looked up. The light from the moon struck his pale face and the black jewel imbedded in his forehead. He regarded Yisselda with melancholy eyes, though his lips tried to smile. "I thank you, Yisselda, for your faith in me, but I fear it *will* need more than Dorian Hawkmoon to win the fight against all Granbretan, and the warrior's perfidy has made me despair the more. . . ."

"There is no proof of perfidy, my dear."

"No—but I knew instinctively that he planned to leave us, taking the machine with him. He sensed my knowledge, too. I do not doubt he has it and is far away by now. I do not necessarily suspect that he takes it for an ignoble purpose. Possibly his purpose is of greater importance than mine, yet I cannot excuse his actions. He deceived me. He betrayed me."

"If he served the Runestaff, he may know more than you. He may wish to preserve this thing, may think it dangerous to you."

"I have no proof he serves the Runestaff. For all I know, he may serve the Dark Empire and I am their tool!"

"You have become oversuspicious, my love."

"I have been forced to become so," Hawkmoon sighed. "I will be so until Granbretan is defeated or I am destroyed." And he held her close to him, burying his weary head in her bosom, and slept that way all night.

In the morning the sun was bright though the air cold. Hawkmoon's gloomy spirits had departed with the deep sleep, and they all appeared in a better mood. All were ravenous, including the mutant beasts, whose tongues lolled and whose eyes were greedy and fierce. Oladahn had fashioned himself a bow and some arrows early and had gone off into the deeper reaches of the forest to seek game.

D'Averc coughed theatrically as he polished his huge boar-helm with a piece of cloth he had found in the bottom of the chariot.

"This western air does not do my weak lungs any good," he said. "I would rather be in the east again, perhaps in Asiacommunista, where I have heard a noble civilization exists. Perhaps such a civilization would appreciate my talents, elevate me to some high estate."

"You have given up hope of any reward from the King-Emperor?" Hawkmoon asked with a grin.

"The reward I'll get is the same he's promised you," D'Averc said mournfully. "If that damned pilot had not lived . . . and then my being seen fighting with you at the castle . . . No, friend Hawkmoon, I am afraid my ambitions as far as Granbretan go are now seen to be somewhat unrealistic."

Oladahn appeared, staggering under the weight of two deer, one on each shoulder. They jumped up to help him.

"Two with two shots," he said proudly. "And the arrows were hastily made at that."

"We cannot eat all of one, let alone two," D'Averc said.

"The beasts," Oladahn said. "They need feeding or I'll warrant, Red Amulet or no Red Amulet, they'll feed on us before the day's done."

They quartered the larger deer and flung it to the mutant cats, who gulped the meat down swiftly, growling softly. Then they set about making a spit on which to roast the second animal.

When they were eating at last, Hawkmoon sighed and smiled. "They say that good food banishes all care," he said, "but I had not believed it until now. I feel a new man. That is the first good meal I have eaten in months. Fresh-killed venison eaten in the woods—ah, the pleasure of it!"

D'Averc, who was wiping his fingers fastidiously and had apparently eaten delicately an enormous amount of meat, said, "I admire health such as yours, Hawkmoon. I wish I had your hearty appetite."

"And I wish I had yours," said Oladahn, laughing, "for you've eaten enough to last you a week."

D'Averc looked at him reproachfully.

Yisselda, who was still wrapped only in Hawkmoon's cloak, shivered a little and put down the bone on which she had been chewing. "I wonder," said she, "if we could seek out a town as soon as possible. There are things I would purchase. . . ."

Hawkmoon looked embarrassed. "Of course, Yisselda, my dear, though it will be difficult. . . . If Dark Empire warriors are thick in these parts, it would be better to drive on farther south and west toward the Kamarg. Perhaps in Carpathia a town can be found. We must be almost upon her borders now."

D'Averc pointed his thumb to the chariot and the beasts. "We'd get a poor reception arriving at a town in that unearthly thing," he said. "Perhaps if one of us went into the nearest settlement . . . ? But then, what would we use for money?"

"I have the Red Amulet," Hawkmoon said. "It could be traded. . . ."

"Fool," said D'Averc, suddenly deadly serious and glaring at him. "That amulet is your life—and ours —our only protection, the only means of controlling our beasts there. It seems to me that it is not the amulet you hate, but the responsibility it implies."

Hawkmoon shrugged. "Maybe. Perhaps I was a fool to suggest it. Still, I like not the thing. I saw what you did not—I saw what it had done to a man who had worn it thirty years."

Oladahn interrupted. "There is no need for this dispute, friends, for I anticipated our need and while you, with great ferocity, were finishing off our foes in the Mad God's hall, Duke Dorian, I dug a few eyes from the Dark Empire men . . ."

"Eyes!" Hawkmoon said in revulsion, then relaxed and smiled as he saw Oladahn holding up a handful of jewels he had prised from the Granbretanians' masks.

"Well," said D'Averc, "we need provisions desperately, and the Lady Yisselda needs some clothing. Who'll stand least chance attracting attention if he goes into a town when we get to Carpathia?"

Hawkmoon gave him a sardonic glance. "Why, you, of course, Sir Huillam, without your Dark Empire accessories. For I, as I am sure you would have pointed out, have this damned black jewel to label me, and

Oladahn has his furry face. But you are still my prisoner. . . ."

"I am aggrieved, Duke Dorian. I thought us allies—united against a common enemy, united by blood, by saving each other's lives. . . ."

"You have not saved mine, as I recall."

"Not specifically, I suppose. Still . . ."

"And I am not disposed to give you a handful of jewels and set you free," Hawkmoon continued, adding in a more somber tone. "Besides, I'm not in a trusting mood today."

"You would have my word, Duke Dorian," D'Averc said lightly, though his eyes seemed to harden slightly.

Hawkmoon frowned.

"He has proved himself our friend in several fights," Oladahn said softly.

Hawkmoon sighed. "Forgive me, D'Averc. Very well, when we reach Carpathia, you will buy us what we need."

D'Averc began to cough. "This damnable air. It will be the death of me."

They rode on, the horned cats loping at a more gentle pace than the previous day's but still making faster speed than any horse. They left the great forest by midday and by evening saw in the distance the mountains of Carpathia at the same time as Yisselda pointed north, indicating the tiny figures of riders approaching them.

"They've seen us," Oladahn said, "and seem to be planning to ride at an angle to cut us off."

Hawkmoon flicked his whip over the flanks of the huge beasts drawing the chariot. "Faster!" he shouted, and almost at once the chariot began to gather speed.

A little later D'Averc called above the rumble and rattle of the wheels, "They're Dark Empire riders—no doubt of that. Order of the Walrus if I'm not mistaken."

"The King-Emperor must be planning a serious invasion of Ukrania," Hawkmoon said. "There's no other reason for so many bands of Dark Empire warriors here. That means he has almost certainly consolidated all conquests farther west and south."

"Save for the Kamarg, I hope," said Yisselda.

The race continued, with the horsemen gradually drawing nearer, riding, as they were, at an angle to the chariot's course.

Hawkmoon smiled grimly, letting the riders think they were catching them. "Ready with your bow, Oladahn," he said. "Here's an opportunity for target practice."

As the horsemen, in grotesque, grinning walrus masks of ebony and ivory, drew close, Oladahn nocked arrow to string and let fly. A rider fell, and a few javelins hurtled toward the chariot but dropped short. Three more members of the Walrus Order died from Oladahn's arrows before they were outdistanced and the jaguars were hauling their burden into the first foothills of the Carpathian Mountains.

Within two hours it was dark and they decided it was safe to camp.

Three days later they contemplated the rocky side of a mountain and knew that they would have to abandon both beasts and chariot if they were to cross the range at all. They would have to travel on foot; there was no alternative.

The terrain had become increasingly difficult for the mutant jaguars, and the mountainside ahead was impossible for them to climb dragging the chariot. They had tried to find a pass, had wasted two days looking for one, but there was none.

Meanwhile, if they were pursued, their pursuers would be almost upon them by now. There was no doubt in their minds that Hawkmoon had been recognized as the man whom the King-Emperor Huon had sworn to destroy. Therefore, Dark Empire warriors, interested in elevating themselves in the eyes of their master, would be eager to seek him out.

So they began to climb, stumbling up the steep face of the mountain, leaving the unharnessed beasts behind them.

When they were nearing a ledge that seemed to extend for some distance around the mountain and offer a relatively easy path, they heard the rattle of weapons and hooves and saw the same walrus-masked riders who had pursued them on the plain come riding from behind some rocks below.

"Their javelins are bound to get us at this range," D'Averc said grimly. "And there's no cover."

But Hawkmoon smiled thinly. "There is still one thing," he said, and raised his voice. "At them, my beasts—kill them, my cats! Obey me, in the name of the amulet!"

The mutant cats turned their baleful eyes on the newcomers, who were so jubilant at seeing their victims exposed that they hardly noticed the horned jaguars. The leader raised his javelin.

And the cats leaped.

Yisselda did not look back as the terrified screams filled the air and the bloodcurdling snarls echoed through the quiet mountains as the Mad God's beasts first killed and then fed.

By the next day they had crossed the mountains and come to a green valley with a little red town that was very peaceful.

D'Averc looked down at the town and held out his hand to Oladahn. "The jewels, if you please, friend Oladahn. By the Runestaff, I feel naked in just shirt and britches!" He took the jewels, tossed them in his palm, winked at Hawkmoon, and set off for the village.

They lay in the grass and watched him walk down whistling and enter the street; then he disappeared.

They waited for four hours. Hawkmoon's face be-

gan to grow grim, and he glanced resentfully at Oladahn, who pursed his lips and shrugged.

And then D'Averc reappeared, but he had others
with him. With a shock, Hawkmoon realized they
were Dark Empire troops. Men of the feared Order of
the Wolf, Baron Meliadus's old order. Had they recognized D'Averc and captured him? But no—on the
contrary, D'Averc seemed quite friendly with them.
He waved, turned on his heel, and began to walk up
the hill to where they were hidden, a large bundle on
his back. Hawkmoon was puzzled, for the wolf masks
had gone back into the village, allowing D'Averc to go
free.

"He can talk, can D'Averc," grinned Oladahn. "He
must have convinced them he was an innocent traveler.
Doubtless the Dark Empire is still using the soft approach in Carpathia."

"Perhaps," said Hawkmoon, not entirely convinced.

When D'Averc came back he flung down his bundle
and pulled it open, displaying several shirts and a pair
of britches, as well as a number of different foodstuffs
—cheeses, bread, sausages, cold meat, and the like.
He handed back most of Oladahn's jewels to him. "I
purchased them relatively cheaply," he said, then
frowned as he saw Hawkmoon's expression. "What is
it, Duke Dorian? Not satisfied? I could not get the Lady
Yisselda a gown, I regret, but the britches and shirt
should fit her."

"Dark Empire men," said Hawkmoon, jerking his
thumb at the village. "You seemed very friendly with
them."

"I was worried, I'll admit," D'Averc said, "but they
seem to be cautious of violence. They are in Carpathia to tell the folk of the benefits of Dark Empire
rule. Apparently the King of Carpathia is entertaining
one of their nobles. The usual technique—gold before
violence. They asked me a few questions but were not
unduly suspicious. They say they're warring in Shekia,

have almost subdued that nation but for a key city or two."

"You did not mention us?" Hawkmoon said.

"Of course not."

Half-satisfied, Hawkmoon relaxed a little.

D'Averc picked up the cloth in which he'd wrapped his bundle. "Look—four cloaks with hoods, such as the holy men in these parts wear. They'll hide our faces well enough. I heard there's a larger town about a day's walk further south. It's a town where they trade horses. We can get there by tomorrow and buy steeds. Is it a good idea?"

Hawkmoon nodded slowly. "Aye. We need horses."

The town was called Zorvanemi, and it bustled with folk of all sorts come to sell and to buy horses. Just outside the main town were the stockyards, and here were many kinds of horseflesh, from thoroughbreds to plow horses.

They arrived too late in the evening to buy, and they put up at an inn on the edge of town, close to the stockyards, so that they could buy what they wanted and be away early in the morning. Here and there they saw small groups of Dark Empire Soldiers, but the soldiers paid no attention to the cowled holy men who mingled with the crowd; there were several deputations from different monasteries in the area, and one more went unnoticed.

In the warmth of the inn's public room they ordered hot wine and food and consulted a map they had bought, speaking softly, discussing their best route through to southern France.

A little later the door of the inn was pushed open, and the cold night air swept in. Over the sounds of conversation and occasional laughter, they heard the coarse tones of a man yelling for wine for himself and his comrades and suggesting to the landlord that girls should be found for them as well.

Hawkmoon glanced up and was instantly on his

guard. The men who had entered were soldiers in the Order of the Boar, the order that D'Averc had belonged to. With their squat, armored bodies and heavy helmet masks, they looked, in the half-light, exactly like the animals they represented, as if so many bores had learned to talk and walk on their hind legs.

The landlord was plainly nervous, clearing his throat several times and asking them what wine they preferred.

"Strong wine, plentiful wine," shouted the leader. "And the same goes for the women. Where are your women? I hope they're lovelier than your horses. Come man, be quick. We've spent all day buying horse-flesh and helping this town's prosperity—now you'll do us a favor."

The boar warriors were evidently here to buy steeds for the Dark Empire troops—probably those bent on conquering Shekia, which lay just across the border.

Hawkmoon, Yisselda, Oladahn, and D'Averc drew their cowls surreptitiously about their heads and sipped at their wine without looking up.

There were three serving wenches in the public room, as well as two men and the landlord himself. As one passed, the boar warrior grabbed her and pressed the snout of his mask against her cheek.

"Give an old pig a kiss, little girl," he roared.

She wriggled and tried to get free, but he held her tight. Now there was silence everywhere else in the tavern, and tension.

"Come outside with me," the boar leader continued. "I'm in a rutting mood."

"Oh, no, please let me go," the girl sobbed. "I'm to be married next week."

"Married, eh?" guffawed the warrior. "Well, let me teach you a thing or two for you to teach your husband."

The girl screamed and continued to resist. No one else in the tavern moved.

"Come on," the warrior said hoarsely. "Outside . . ."

"I won't," wept the girl. "I won't until I'm married."

"Is that all?" The boar-masked man laughed. "Well, then—I'll marry you if that's what you want." He turned suddenly and glared at the four who sat in the shadows. "You're holy men, aren't you? One of you can marry us." And before Hawkmoon and the rest had realized what was happening, he had grabbed Yisselda, who sat on the outside of the bench, and hauled her to her feet. "Marry us, holy man, or—By the Runestaff! What sort of a holy man are you?" Yisselda's cowl had fallen back, revealing her lovely hair.

Hawkmoon stood up. There was nothing for it now but to fight. Oladahn and D'Averc stood up.

As one, they drew the swords hidden under their robes. As one, they launched themselves at the armored warriors, yelling for the women to flee.

The boar warriors were drunk and surprised, and the three companions were neither. It was their only advantage. Hawkmoon's blade slipped between breastplate and gorget of the leader and killed him before he could draw his own sword, while Oladahn's swipe to another's barely protected legs hamstrung him. D'Averc managed to slice off the hand of one who had stripped off his gauntlets.

Now they fought back and forth across the tavern floor as men and women made hastily for the stairs and doors, many to crowd to the gallery above to watch.

Oladahn, forsaking normal swordplay in the narrow room, had leaped onto the back of a huge opponent and, dirk in hand, was trying to stab him through the eyeholes of his mask while the man clumsily tried to dislodge him, staggering about half-blind.

D'Averc was fencing with a swordsman of some skill who was driving him back steadily toward the stairs, while Hawkmoon was desperately defending himself against a man with a huge axe that, every time it missed him, chopped chunks out of the woodwork.

Hawkmoon, hampered by his cloak, was trying to get out of it and at the same time duck the blows from the axe. He stepped to one side, tripped in the folds of the cloak, and fell. Above, the axeman snorted and raised the axe for the final blow.

Hawkmoon rolled just in time as the axe came down and sheared through the cloth of his gown. He leaped up as he tugged the axe from the hard wood of the floor and swung his sword round to clang against the back of the axeman's neck. The man groaned and fell, dazed, to his knees. Hawkmoon kicked back the mask, revealing a red twisted face, and stabbed into the gaping mouth, driving the sword deep into the throat so that the jugular was cut and blood shot from the helm. Hawkmoon withdrew his blade and the helm clanged shut.

Nearby, Oladahn was struggling, half-off his man, who had now got a grip on his arm and was tugging him away from his neck. Hawkmoon jumped forward and with both hands drove his sword into the man's belly, piercing armor, leather underjerkin, and flesh. The man screamed and crumpled to the floor, to lie there writhing.

Then together Oladahn and Hawkmoon took D'Averc's man from behind, both swords slashing at him, until he, too, lay dead on the floor.

There was nothing left but to finish off the handless man who lay propped against a bench, weeping and trying to stick his hand back on.

Panting, Hawkmoon looked about the tavern room at the carnage they had wrought. "Not a bad night's work for holy men," he said.

D'Averc looked thoughtful. "Maybe," he said softly, "it is time to change our disguise to a more useful one."

"What do you mean?"

"There are enough pieces of boar armor here to furnish all four of us, particularly since I still have mine. I speak the secret language of the Order of the

Boar. With luck we could travel disguised as those we fear most—as Dark Empire men. We have been wondering how to get through the countries where Granbretan has consolidated her gains. Well—here's our way."

Hawkmoon thought deeply. D'Averc's suggestion was a wild one, but it had possibilities, particularly since D'Averc himself knew all the rituals of the order.

"Aye," said Hawkmoon. "Perhaps you're right, D'Averc. We could then go where the Dark Empire forces are thickest and stand a chance of getting to the Kamarg faster. Very well, we'll do it."

They began stripping the armor from the corpses.

"We can be sure of the landlord's and townspeople's silence," said D'Averc, "for they'll not want it known that six Dark Empire warriors were killed here."

Oladahn watched them work, nursing his twisted arm. "A pity," he said with a sigh. "It was an exploit that should be recorded."

Chapter Eight

THE DARK EMPIRE CAMP

"BROOD OF THE Mountain Giants! I'll stifle to death before we've gone a mile!" The muffled voice of Oladahn came from within the grotesque helmet as he tried to tug himself free of its engulfing weight. They sat, all four, in their room above the tavern, trying on the captured armor.

Hawkmoon, too, was finding the stuff uncomfortable. Apart from the fact that it did not fit him properly, it made him feel distinctly claustrophobic. He had worn something like it some time before, when disguised in the wolf armor of Baron Meliadus's order, but if anything, the boar armor was even heavier and far less comfortable. It must be that much worse for Yisselda.

Only D'Averc was used to it and had donned his own, to look with some relish and amusement at their first encounter with the uniform of his order.

"No wonder you claim ill health," Hawkmoon told him. "I know of nothing less healthy. I'm tempted to forget the whole plan."

"You'll become more used to it as we ride," D'Averc assured him. "A little chaffing, a little stuffiness; then you'll find you'll feel naked without it."

"I'd rather be naked," Oladahn protested, yanking off the leering boar mask at last. It fell with a clatter to the floor.

"Careful with it," D'Averc wagged a finger. "We don't want to damage any more."

Oladahn gave the helmet an extra kick.

A day and a night later, they were riding deep into Shekia. There was no doubt that the Dark Empire had conquered the province, for towns and villages were everywhere laid waste, crucified corpses hung along every road, carrion birds were thick in the air and even thicker on the ground where they feasted. The night had been as light as if the sun were permanently on the horizon, lit by the funeral pyres of villages, farms, towns, villas, and cities. And the black hordes of the Island Empire of Granbretan, brands in one hand, swords in the other, rode like demons from hell, howling and shrieking across the broken land.

Survivors hid, cringing from the four as they rode in disguise through this world of terror, galloping as fast as they could, for none suspected them. They were just one small pack of murderers and looters among many, and neither friend nor foe had any suspicion of their real identities.

Now it was morning, a morning overcast with black smoke, warmed by distant fires, a morning of ash-covered fields and trampled crops, of broken flowers and bloody corpses, a morning like any other morning in a land under the heel of Granbretan.

Along the churned mud of the road, a group of riders came toward them, swathed in great canvas night cloaks that covered their bemasked heads as well as their bodies. They rode powerful black horses and were hunched in their saddles as if they had been riding for many days.

As they drew close, Hawkmoon murmured, "Dark Empire men for certain, and they seem to be taking an interest in us. . . ."

The leader pushed back his canvas cowl and revealed a huge boar mask, larger and more ornate than even D'Averc's. He reined in his black stallion, and his men came to a halt behind him.

"Silence, all three," murmured D'Averc, leading them up to the waiting warriors. "I'll speak."

Now from the leader of the boar warriors came a peculiar snorting, snuffling, and whining voice that must be speaking, thought Hawkmoon, the secret language of the Order of the Boar.

He was surprised to hear similar sounds begin to issue from D'Averc's throat. The conversation continued for some time, D'Averc pointing back down the road, the boar leader jerking his helm mask in the other direction. Then the leader urged his horse on, and he and his men filed past the nervous three and continued on up the road.

"What did he want?" Hawkmoon asked.

"Wanted to know if we'd seen any livestock. They're a foraging party of some sort, out to locate provisions for the camp ahead."

"What camp's that?"

"A big one, he said, about four miles further on. They're getting ready to attack one of the last cities still standing against them—Bradichla. I know the place. It had beautiful architecture."

"Then we are close to Osterland," Yisselda said, "and beyond Osterland lies Italia, and beyond Italia, Provence . . . home."

"True," said D'Averc. "Your geography is excellent. But we are not home yet, and the most dangerous part of the journey has still to be encountered."

"What shall we do about this camp," Oladahn said, "skirt it or try to ride through it?"

"It's a vast camp," D'Averc told him. "Our best chance would be to go through the middle, possibly even spend the night in it and try to learn something of the Dark Empire's plans—whether they have heard we are nearby, for instance."

Hawkmoon's muffled voice came from the helmet. "I am not sure it is not too dangerous," he said doubtfully. "Yet if we try to skirt the camp, we might arouse suspicion. Very well, we go through it."

"Will we not have to remove our masks, Dorian?" Yisselda asked him.

"No fear of that," D'Averc said. "The native Granbretanian often sleeps in his mask, hates to reveal his face."

Hawkmoon had noticed the weariness in Yisselda's voice and knew that they must rest soon; it would have to be in the Granbretanian camp.

They had expected the camp to be huge, but not as vast as this. In the distance beyond it was the walled city of Bradichla, its spires and façades visible even from here.

"They are remarkably beautiful," said D'Averc with a sigh. He shook his head. "What a pity they must fall tomorrow. They were fools to resist this army."

"It is of incredible size," said Oladahn. "Surely unnecessary to defeat that town?"

"The Dark Empire aims at speed of conquest," Hawkmoon told him. "I have seen larger armies than this used on smaller cities. But the camp covers a great distance, and organization will not be perfect. I think we can hide here."

There were canopies, tents, even huts built here and there, cooking fires on which food of all descriptions was being prepared, and corrals for horses, bullocks, and mules. Slaves hauled great war machines through the mud of the camp, goaded on by men of the Order of the Ant. Banners fluttered in the breeze, and the standards of a score of military orders were stuck here and there in the ground. From a distance, it seemed like some primeval concourse of beasts as a line of wolves tramped across a ruined field or a gathering of moles (one of the engineering orders) groaned about a cooking fire, while elsewhere could be seen wasps, ravens, ferrets, rats, foxes, tigers, boars, flies, hounds, badgers, goats, wolverines, otters, and even a few mantises, select guards whose Grand Constable was King Huon himself.

Hawkmoon himself recognized several of the banners—that of Adaz Prompt, fat Grand Constable of the Order of the Hound; Brenal Farnu's ornate flag, showing him to be a Baron of Granbretan and the Rats' Grand Constable; the fluttering standard of Shenegar Trott, Count of Sussex. Hawkmoon guessed that this city must be the last to fall in a sustained campaign and that was why the army was so large and attended by so many high-ranking warlords. He made out Shenegar Trott himself, being borne in a horse litter toward his tent, his robes covered in jewels, his pale silver mask wrought in the parody of a human face.

Shenegar Trott seemed like a soft-living, soft-brained aristocrat, ruined by rich living, but Hawkmoon had seen Shenegar Trott do battle at the Ford of Weizna on the Rhine, had seen him deliberately sink himself and horse under water and ride along the river bottom, to emerge on the enemy's bank. It was the puzzling thing about all Dark-Empire noblemen. They seemed soft, lazy, and self-indulgent; yet they were as strong as the beasts they pretended to be and were often braver. Shenegar Trott was also the man who had hacked off the limb of a screaming child and eaten a bite from it while its mother was forced to watch.

"Well," said Hawkmoon, taking a deep breath, "let's ride through and camp as near to the far side as we can. I hope we'll be able to slip away in the morning."

They rode slowly through the camp. From time to time a boar would greet them and D'Averc would answer for them. Eventually they came to the farthest edge of the camp and dismounted. They had brought the gear stolen from the men they had killed in the tavern, and now they set it up without suspicion, for it bore no special insignia. D'Averc watched the others work. It would not do, he had told them, for one of his obvious rank to be seen helping his men.

A group of engineers of the Badger Order came tramping around with a cartload of spare axeheads, sword pommels, arrowheads, spear tips, and the like. They also had a sharpening machine.

"Any work for us, brother boars?" they grunted, pausing beside the little camp.

Hawkmoon boldly drew his blunted blade. "This needs sharpening."

"Aye, and I've lost a bow and a quiver of arrows," Oladahn said, eyeing a batch of bows in the bottom of the cart.

"What about your mate?" said the man in the badger mask. "He's got no sword at all." He indicated Yisselda.

"Then give him one, fool," barked D'Averc in his most lordly tone, and the badger hastily obeyed.

When they had been reequipped and had their weapons freshly sharpened. Hawkmoon felt his confidence come back. He was pleased at the coolness of his deception.

Only Yisselda seemed downhearted. She hefted the great sword she had been forced to strap around her waist. "Much more weight," she said, "and I'll fall to my knees."

"Best get inside the tent," Hawkmoon said, "there you'll be able to take off some of the gear, at least."

D'Averc seemed unsettled, watching Hawkmoon and Oladahn prepare a cooking fire.

"What ails you, D'Averc?" Hawkmoon asked, looking up and peering through the eyeslits of his helmet. "Sit down. The food will not be long."

"I smell something wrong," D'Averc murmured. "I am not altogether happy that we are in no danger."

"Why? Do you think the badgers suspected us?"

"Not at all." D'Averc looked across the camp. Evening darkened the sky, and the warriors were beginning to settle down; there was less movement now. On the walls of the distant city, soldiers lined the battlements, ready to resist an army that none had resisted to date, save for the Kamarg. "Not at all," D'Averc repeated, half to himself, "but I would feel relieved if . . ."

"If what?"

"I think I will walk about the camp a little, see what gossip I can hear."

"Is that wise? Besides, if we are approached by others of the Boar Order, we'll not be able to speak the language."

"I'll not be gone long. Get into your tents as soon as you can."

Hawkmoon wanted to stop D'Averc, but he did not know how to without attracting unwanted attention. He watched D'Averc stride off through the camp.

Just then a voice said from behind them, "A nice-looking piece of sausage you have there, brothers."

Hawkmoon turned. It was a warrior in the mask of the Order of the Wolf.

"Aye," said Oladahn quickly. "Aye—will you have a piece . . . brother?" He cut a slice of sausage and handed it to the man in the wolf mask. The warrior turned, lifted his mask, popped the food into his mouth, lowered his mask quickly, and turned back again.

"Thanks," he said. "I've been traveling for days on next to nothing. Our commander drives you hard. We just came in. Riding faster than a flying Frenchman." He laughed. "All the way from Provence."

"From Provence?" Hawkmoon said involuntarily.

"Aye. Been there?"

"Once or twice. Have we won the Kamarg yet?"

"As good as. Commander thinks it's a matter of days. They're virtually leaderless, running out of provisions. Those weapons they've got have killed a million of us, but they won't kill many more before we ride over them!"

"What happened to Count Brass, their leader?"

"Dead, I heard—or as good as. Their morale's getting worse every day. By the time we get back, I should think it'll be all over there. I'll be glad. I've been pitched there for months. This is the first change of scenery since we began the damned campaign. Thanks for the sausage, brothers. Good killing tomorrow!"

Hawkmoon watched the wolf warrior stamp away into the night that was now lit by a thousand campfires. He sighed and entered the tent. "You heard that?" he asked Yisselda.

"I heard." She had removed her helmet and greaves and was combing her hair. "It seems my father still lives." She spoke in an overcontrolled tone, and Hawkmoon, even in the darkness of the tent, could see tears in her eyes.

He took her face in his hands and said, "Do not fear, Yisselda. A few days more and we shall be at his side."

"If he lives that long . . ."

"He awaits us. He will live."

Later Hawkmoon went outside. Oladahn sat by the dying fire, arms around his knees.

"D'Averc has been gone too long," said Oladahn.

"Aye," said Hawkmoon distantly, staring at the faraway walls of the city. "Has he came to harm? I wonder."

"Deserted us, more likely—" Oladahn broke off as several figures emerged from the shadows.

Hawkmoon saw, with sinking heart, that they were boar-masked warriors. "Into your tent, quickly," he murmured to Oladahn.

But it was too late. One of the boars was already talking to Hawkmoon, addressing him in the guttural secret tongue of the order. Hawkmoon nodded and raised a hand as if acknowledging a greeting, hoping that that was all it was, but the boar's tone became more insistent. Hawkmoon tried to enter his tent, but an arm restrained him.

Again the boar spoke to him. Hawkmoon coughed, pretending illness, pointing at his throat. But then the boar said, "I asked you, *brother,* if you drink with us. Take off that mask!"

Hawkmoon knew that no member of any order would demand of another that he remove his mask— unless he suspected him of wearing it illicitly. He stepped back and drew his sword.

"I regret I should not like to drink with you, *brother.* But I'll happily fight with you."

Oladahn sprang up beside him, his own sword ready.

"Who are you?" growled the boar. "Why wear the armor of another order? What sense does that make?"

Hawkmoon flung back his helm, revealing his pale face and the black jewel that shone there. "I am Hawkmoon," he said simply, and leaped forward into the mass of astonished warriors.

The pair took the lives of five of the Dark Empire men before the noise of the fight brought others running from all over the camp. Riders galloped up. All around him Hawkmoon was aware of shouts and the babble of voices. His arm rose and fell in the darkness of the press, but soon it was gripped by a dozen hands and he felt himself borne down. A spear haft caught him a buffet in the back of his neck, and he fell into the mud of the field.

Dazed, he was dragged upright and hauled before a

tall, black-armored figure seated on a horse some distance away from the main mass. His mask was lifted back, and he peered up at the horseman.

"Ah, this is pleasant, Duke of Köln," came the deep, musical voice from within the horseman's helm, a voice edged with evil and with malice; a voice Hawkmoon recognized dimly but could not believe in his recognition.

"My long journey has not been wasted," said the horseman, turning to his mounted companion.

"I am glad, my lord," was the reply. "I trust I am now reinstated in the eyes of the King-Emperor?"

Hawkmoon's head jerked up to look at the other man. His eyes blazed as he recognized the elaborate mask-helm of D'Averc.

Thickly, Hawkmoon cried, "So you have betrayed us? Another betrayal! Are all men traitors to Hawkmoon's cause?" He tried to break free, to grab with his hands at D'Averc, but the warriors held him back.

D'Averc laughed. "You are naïve, Duke Dorian. . . ." He began to cough weakly.

"Have you got the others?" the horseman asked. "The girl and the little beast-man?"

"Aye, your excellency," answered one of the men.

"Then bring them to my camp. I want to inspect them all closely. This is a very satisfying day for me."

Chapter Nine

THE JOURNEY SOUTH

A STORM HAD begun to rumble over the camp as Hawkmoon, Oladahn, and Yisselda were dragged through the mud and the filth, past the bright, curious eyes of the warriors, through the noise and confusion, to where a great banner fluttered in the newly come wind.

Lightning suddenly split a jagged gulf in the sky, and thunder growled, then exploded. More lightning came, fast on the thunder's heels, illuminating the scene before them. Hawkmoon gasped as he recognized the banner, tried to speak to Oladahn or Yisselda, but was then bundled into a large pavilion where a masked man sat on a carved chair, D'Averc standing beside him. The man in the chair wore the mask of the Order of the Wolf. The banner had proclaimed him Grand Constable of that order, one of the greatest nobles in all Granbretan, First Chieftain of the Armies of the Dark Empire under the King-Emperor Huon, a Baron of Kroiden—a man Hawkmoon thought dead, was sure he had slain him himself.

"Baron Meliadus!" he grunted. "You did not die at Hamadan."

"No, I did not die, Hawkmoon, though you wounded me sorely. I escaped that battlefield."

Hawkmoon smiled thinly. "Few of your men did. We defeated you—routed you."

Meliadus turned his ornate wolf mask and spoke to a captain who stood nearby. "Bring chains. Bring many chains, strong and of great weight. Heap them on these dogs and rivet them. I want no locks that might be picked. This time I will be sure they are brought to Granbretan."

He left his chair and descended, to peer through the eyeslits in his mask at Hawkmoon's face. "They have discussed you often at King Huon's Court, have devised such exquisite, such elaborate, such splendid punishments for you, traitor. Your dying will take a year or two, and each moment will be agony of mind, spirit, and body. All our ingenuity, Hawkmoon, we have squandered on you."

He stepped back and reached out a black gauntlet to cup Yisselda's hate-twisted face. She turned her head, eyes filled with anger and despair. "And as for you—I offered you all honors to become my wife. Now you will have no honor, but a husband I shall be to you until I tire of you or your body breaks." The wolf head moved slowly to regard Oladahn. "And as for this creature, unhuman, yet upstart enough to walk on two legs, he shall crawl and whine like the animal he is, be trained to behave like a proper beast. . . ."

Oladahn spat at the jeweled mask. "I'll have an excellent model in you," he said.

Meliadus whirled, cloak swirling, and limped heavily back to his chair.

"I'll save all until we've presented ourselves at the throne globe," Meliadus said, his voice slightly unsteady. "I've been patient and will remain so for a few more days. We move off at first light, returning to Granbretan. But we shall take a slight detour in order that you may witness the final destruction of the Kamarg. I have been there for a month, you know, and watched its men die daily, watched the towers fall, one by one. There are not many left. I have told them to hold off the last assault until I return. I thought you would like to see your homeland . . . raped." He laughed, putting his grotesquely masked head on one side to look at them again. "Ah! Here are the chains."

Members of the Order of the Badger were coming in, bearing huge iron chains, a brazier, hammers, and rivets.

Hawkmoon, Yisselda, and Oladahn struggled as the badgers bound them, but soon they were forced down to the floor by the weight of the iron links.

Then the red-hot rivet nails were hammered home, and Hawkmoon knew that no human being could possibly hope to escape such bonds.

Baron Meliadus came to look down at him when the work was done. "We'll journey by land to the Kamarg and from there to Bordeaux, where a ship will be waiting for us. I regret I cannot offer you a flying machine—we are using most of them to level the Kamarg."

Hawkmoon closed his eyes; the only gesture he could make to display his contempt for his captor.

Bundled into an open wagon the next morning, the three were given no food before Baron Meliadus's heavily guarded caravan set off. From time to time Hawkmoon caught a glimpse of his enemy, riding near the head of the column with Sir Huillam d'Averc by his side.

The weather was still stormy and oppressive, and a few heavy drops of rain splashed on Hawkmoon's face and fell into his eyes. He was so heavily bound that he could barely shake his head to rid it of the moisture.

The wagon bumped and jerked away, and in the distance the Dark Empire troops were marching against the city.

It seemed to Hawkmoon that he had been betrayed on all sides. He had trusted the Warrior in Jet and Gold and had had his saddlebags stolen; he had trusted D'Averc and found himself delivered into the hands of Baron Meliadus. Now he sighed, not sure that even Oladahn would not betray him, given the opportunity. . . .

He found himself slipping almost comfortably into the mood that had possessed him months before after his defeat and capture by Granbretan when he had led an army against Baron Meliadus in Germany. His face became frozen, his eyes dull, and he ceased to think.

Sometimes Yisselda would speak and he would answer with an effort, having no words of comfort because he knew that there were none that would convince her. Sometimes Oladahn would try to make a cheerful comment, but the others did not reply, and eventually he, too, lapsed into silence. Only when, from time to time, food was pushed into their mouths did they show any signs of life.

So the days passed as the caravan trundled southward towards the Kamarg.

They had all anticipated this homecoming for months, but now they looked forward to it without joy. Hawkmoon knew he had failed in his chosen mission, failed to save the Kamarg, and he was full of self-contempt.

Soon they were passing through Italia, and Baron Meliadus called out one day, "The Kamarg we'll reach before a couple of nights have passed. We are just crossing the border into France!" And he laughed.

Chapter Ten

THE FALL OF THE KAMARG

"SIT THEM UP," said Baron Meliadus, "so they can see."

On horseback, he leaned over to look into the wagon. "Get them up straight," he told his sweating men who were wrestling with the three bodies still clad in armor and made heavier by the great weight of chains about them. "They do not look well," he added. "And I thought them such hardy spirits!"

D'Averc rode up beside Baron Meliadus, coughing, hunched a little in his saddle. "And you're still in poor condition, D'Averc. Did not my apothecary mix you the medicine you asked for?"

"He did, my lord Baron," D'Averc said weakly, "but it does me little good."

"It should have done, the mixture of herbs you had him put in it." Meliadus returned his attention to the three prisoners. "See, we have stopped on this hill so that you could look at your homeland."

Hawkmoon blinked in the midday sunlight, recognizing the marshlands of his beloved Kamarg stretching and shining away to the horizon.

But closer he saw the great, somber watchtowers of the Kamarg, the strength of the Kamarg with their strange weapons of incredible power, whose secrets were known only to Count Brass. And camped near them, a black mass of men, like so many million ants ready to sweep in, were the gathered forces of the Dark Empire.

"Oh!" sobbed Yisselda. "They can never withstand so many!"

"An intelligent estimate, my dear," said Baron Meliadus. "You are quite right."

He and his party had come to a rest on the slopes of a hill that led gradually down to the plain where the troops of Granbretan massed. Hawkmoon could see infantry, cavalry, engineers, rank upon rank of them; he saw war engines of enormous size, huge flame canon, ornithopters flapping through the skies in such numbers that they blotted out the sun as they passed over the heads of the onlookers. All manner of metal had been brought against the peaceful Kamarg, brass and iron and bronze and steel, tough alloys that could resist the bite of the flame-lance, gold and silver and platinum and lead. Vultures marched beside frogs, and horses beside moles; there were wolves and boars and stags and wildcats, eagles and ravens and badgers and weasels. Silk banners fluttered in the moist, warm air, bright with the colors of two score of nobles from all corners of Granbretan. There were yellows and purples and blacks and reds, blues and greens and flashing pink, and the sun caught the jewels of a hundred thousand eyes and made them flash, malevolent and grim.

"Aha," laughed Baron Meliadus. "That army *I* command. If Count Brass had not refused to aid us that day, you would all be honoured allies of the Dark Empire of Granbretan. But because you resisted us— you will be punished. You thought your weapons and your towers and the stoic bravery of your men was enough to stand against the might of Granbretan. Not enough, Dorian Hawkmoon, not enough! See—*my* army, raised by me to commit *my* vengeance. See,

Hawkmoon, and know what a fool you and the rest were!" He flung back his head and laughed for a long time. "Tremble, Hawkmoon—and you, too, Yisselda —tremble as your fellows are trembling now within their towers, for they know those towers must fall, they know the Kamarg will be ashes and mud before tomorrow's sunset. I will destroy the Kamarg if it means sacrificing my entire army!"

And Hawkmoon and Yisselda did tremble, though it was with grief at the threat of the destruction foreseen by mad Baron Meliadus.

"Count Brass is dead," said Baron Meliadus, turning his horse to ride to the head of his company, "and now dies the Kamarg!" He waved his arm, "Forward. Let them see the carnage!"

The wagon began to move again, bumping down the hill road to the plain, its prisoners propped in it with stricken faces and miserable eyes.

D'Averc continued to ride beside the wagon coughing ostentatiously. "The Baron's medicine's not bad," he said at length. "It should cure the ills of all his men." And with that enigmatic pronouncement he urged his horse into a gallop to reach the head of the column and ride beside his master.

Hawkmoon saw strange rays flash from the towers of the Kamarg and strike into the gathered ranks that came against them, leaving scars of smoking ground where men had been. He saw the cavalry of the Kamarg begin to move up to take its positions, a thin line of battered Guardians, riding their horned horses, flame-lances on their shoulders. He saw ordinary townsfolk from the settlements, armed with swords and axes, coming in the wake of the cavalry. But he did not see Count Brass, he did not see von Villach, and he did not see the philosopher Bowgentle. The men of the Kamarg marched leaderless to this last battle.

He heard the faint sounds of their battle shouts, coming over the howls and roars of the attackers, the crack of cannon and the shriek of flame-lances; heard the clatter of armour and the creak of metal; smelled beast and man and weapon, marching through the mud. And then he saw the black hordes pause as a wall of fire rose into the air before them and scarlet flamingoes flew over it, riders aiming flame-lances at the clanking ornithopters.

Hawkmoon ached to be free, to have the feel of a sword in his hand and a horse between his legs, to rally the men of the Kamarg, who, even leaderless, could still resist the Dark Empire, though their numbers were a fraction of the enemy's. He writhed in his chains, and he cursed in his fury and frustration.

Evening came, and the battle went on. Hawkmoon saw an ancient black tower struck by a million flames from the Dark Empire cannon, saw it sway, topple, and fall, crashing down to become rubble suddenly. And the black hordes cheered.

Night fell, and the battle went on. The heat of it reached even to the three in the wagon and brought sweat to their faces. Around them the wolf guards sat laughing and talking, certain of victory. Their master had ridden his horse into the thick of his troops, the better to see how the battle went, and they brought out a skin of wine with long straws jutting from it so that they could suck the stuff through their masks. As the night grew longer, their talk and their laughter subsided until, strangely, they all slept.

Oladahn remarked on it. "Not like the vigilant wolves to sleep so hard. They must be confident."

Hawkmoon sighed. "Aye, but it does us no good. These damned chains are riveted so fast that we have no hope of escaping."

"What's this?" the voice was D'Averc's. "No longer optimistic, Hawkmoon? I find it hard to believe!"

"Away with you, D'Averc," Hawkmoon said as the man emerged from the darkness to stand beside the wagon. "Back to lick the boots of your master."

"I had brought this," D'Averc said in a mock-aggrieved tone, "to see if it would serve you." He displayed a bulky object in his hand. "After all, it was my medicine that drugged the guards."

Hawkmoon's eyes narrowed. "What's that in your hand?"

"A rarity I found on the battleground. Some great commander's I'd judge, for there are few of them to be found these days. It's a kind of flame-lance, though small enough to be carried in one hand."

"I've heard of them," Hawkmoon nodded. "But what use is it to me? I'm in chains, as you see."

"Aye, I noted that. If you'd take a risk, however, it might be that I could release you."

"Is this a new trap, D'Averc, that you and Meliadus have concocted between you?"

"I'm hurt, Hawkmoon. Why should you think that?"

"Because you betrayed us into Meliadus's hands. You must have prepared the trap well ahead, when you spoke to those wolf warriors in that Carpathian village. You sent them to find their master and arranged to lead us to that camp where we could be most easily captured."

"Why, it sounds possible," agreed D'Averc. "Though you could see it another way—the wolf warriors recognized me then and followed us, going later to warn their master. I heard the rumor at the camp that Meliadus had come to find you, decided to tell Meliadus I had led you into this trap so that one of us would be free at least." D'Averc paused. "How does that sound?"

"Glib."

"Well, yes, it does sound glib. Now, Hawkmoon, there is not much time. Shall I see if I can burn your chains without burning you, or would you rather keep your seats for fear of missing a development in the battle?"

"Burn the damned chains," Hawkmoon said, "for at least with my hands free I'll have a chance to choke you if you lie!"

D'Averc brought the little flame-lance up and directed it at an angle to Hawkmoon's fettered arms. Then he touched a stud, and a beam of intense heat sprang from the muzzle. Hawkmoon felt pain sear his arm, but he gritted his teeth. The pain got worse until he felt he must cry out, and then there was a clatter as one of the links fell to the bottom of the wagon and he felt some of the weight leave him. An arm was free, his right arm. He rubbed it and almost yelled as he touched a part where the armour had been burned clean through.

"Hurry," murmured D'Averc. "Here, hold up another length of chain. It will be easier now."

At last Hawkmoon was free of the chain, and they set about releasing Yisselda and then Oladahn. D'Averc was becoming noticeably more nervous by the time they had finished.

"I have your swords here," he said, "and new masks and horses. You must follow me. And hurry, before Meliadus comes back. I had, to tell you the truth, expected him before now."

They crept through the darkness to where the horses were tethered, donned the masks, strapped the swords to their waists, and climbed into their saddles.

Then they heard other steeds galloping up the hill road toward them, heard confused shouts and an angry bellow that could only be Meliadus's.

"Quick," D'Averc hissed. "We must ride—ride for the Kamarg!"

They kicked their horses into a wild gallop and began to career down the hill toward the main battlefield. "Make way!" D'Averc screamed. "Make way! The force must move through. Reinforcements for the front!"

Men leaped aside for their horses as they thundered through the thick of the camp, cursing the four figures who rode so heedlessly.

"Make way!" D'Averc yelled. "A message for the Grand Commander!" He found time to turn his head and call to Hawkmoon, "It bores me to sustain the same lie!" He yelled again, "Make way! The potion for the plague-struck!"

Behind them they heard other horses as Meliadus and his men came in pursuit.

Ahead they could now see that the fighting still continued, but not with the intensity it had had earlier.

"Make way!" bellowed D'Averc. "Make way for Baron Meliadus!"

The horses leaped knots of men, swept around war engines, galloped through fires, drawing nearer and nearer to the Kamarg's towers, while behind them they could hear Meliadus yelling.

Now they reached a point where the horses galloped over corpses, the fallen of Granbretan, and the main force was now behind them.

"Get the masks off," D'Averc called. "It's our only chance. If the Kamargians recognize you and Yisselda in time, they'll hold their fire. If not . . ."

From out of the darkness came the bright beam of a flame-lance, narrowly missing D'Averc. Behind them other flame-lances shot their searing death, aimed doubtless by Meliadus's men. Hawkmoon grappled with the straps of his mask helm, managed at last to unloose it and fling it behind him.

"Stop!" the voice was Meliadus's, gaining on them now. "You'll perish by your own forces! Fools!"

More flame-lances had opened up from the Kamarg side, illuminating the night with ruddy light. The horses rode over the dead, finding it hard going. D'Averc had his head down over his horse's neck, and Yisselda and Oladahn were crouching low, too, but Hawkmoon drew his sword and yelled, "Men of the Kamarg! It is Hawkmoon! Hawkmoon has returned!"

The flame-lances did not cease, but they were getting closer and closer to one of the towers now. D'Averc straightened in his saddle.

"Kamargians! I bring you Hawkmoon, who will—" and fire splashed him. He flung up his arms, cried out, and began to topple from his saddle. Hawkmoon hastily drew alongside, steadying the body. The armor was red-hot, melted in places, but D'Averc seemed not wholly dead. A faint laugh came from the blistered lips. "A piece of serious misjudgment, linking my fortunes with yours, Hawkmoon. . . ."

The other two came to a halt, their horses stamping in confusion. Behind them, Baron Meliadus and his men drew closer.

"Take the reins of his horse, Oladahn," Hawkmoon said. "I'll steady him in his saddle, and we'll see if we can get closer to the tower."

Flame shot out again, this time from the Granbretanian side. "Stop, Hawkmoon!"

Hawkmoon ignored the command and moved on, slowly picking his way through the mud and death all around him, trying to support D'Averc.

Hawkmoon shouted as a great beam of light sprang from the tower. "Men of the Kamarg! It is Hawkmoon—and Yisselda, Count Brass's daughter."

The light faded. Closer now came the horses of Meliadus. Yisselda, too, was swaying in her saddle from exhaustion. Hawkmoon prepared to meet the wolves of Meliadus.

Then, bursting down an incline, streamed a score of armored Guardians, the white, horned horses of the Kamarg under them, and they surrounded the four.

One of the Guardians peered closely into Hawkmoon's face, then his eyes lit with joy. "It is my lord Hawkmoon! It is Yisselda! Ah—now our luck will change!"

Some distance away Meliadus and his men had paused when they saw the Kamargians. Then they turned and rode into the darkness.

They came to Castle Brass in the morning, when the pale sunlight fell on the lagoons and wild bulls looked up from where they drank and watched them pass. A wind stirred the reeds, making them roll like the sea, and the hill overlooking the town was rich with grapes and other fruits just beginning to ripen. On top of the hill stood Castle Brass, solid and old and seemingly unchanged by the wars that had raged on the borders of the province it protected.

They rode up the curling white road to the castle, crossed into the courtyard, where joyous stewards rushed out to take their horses, then entered the hall, which was full of Count Brass's trophies. It was strangely cold and silent, and a single figure stood by the great fireplace waiting for them. Although he smiled, his eyes were fearful and his face had aged much since Hawkmoon had last seen him—wise Sir Bowgentle, the philosopher-poet.

Bowgentle embraced Yisselda, then gripped Hawkmoon's hand.

"How is Count Brass?" Hawkmoon asked.

"Physically well, but he has lost the will to live." Bowgentle signed for stewards to help D'Averc. "Take him to the room in the northern tower—the sickroom. I'll attend to him as soon as I can. Come," he said. "See for yourselves. . . ."

They left Oladahn to stay with D'Averc and climbed the old stone staircase to the landing where Count Brass's apartments still were. Bowgentle opened a door and they entered the bedroom.

There was a simple soldier's bed, big and square, with white sheets and plain pillows. On the pillows lay a great head that seemed carved from metal. The red hair had a little more gray, the bronzed face was a trifle paler, but the red moustache was the same. And the heavy brow that hung like a ledge of rock over the cave of the deepset golden brown eyes, that, too, was the same. But the eyes stared at the ceiling without blinking, and the lips did not move, were set in a hard line.

"Count Brass," murmured Bowgentle. "Look."

But the eyes remained fixed. Hawkmoon had to

come forward, peer straight into the face, and make Yisselda do likewise. "Count Brass, your daughter, Yisselda, has returned, and Dorian Hawkmoon, too."

From the lips now came a rumbling murmur, "More illusions. I'd thought the fever past, Bowgentle."

"So it is, my lord—these are not phantoms."

The eyes moved now to look at them. "Am I dead at last and joined with you, my children?"

"You are on earth, Count Brass!" Hawkmoon said.

Yisselda bent and kissed her father on the lips. "There, father—an earthly kiss."

Gradually the hard line of the lips began to melt, until a smile was there, then a wide grin. Then the body heaved under the clothes, and suddenly Count Brass was sitting upright. "Ah! It's true. I'd lost hope! Fool that I am, I'd lost hope!" He laughed now, suddenly alive with vitality.

Bowgentle was astonished. "Count Brass—I thought you but a pace from the door of death!"

"So I was, Bowgentle—but I've leaped back from it, as you see. Leaped a long way. How goes the siege, Hawkmoon?"

"Badly for us, Count Brass, but better, I'll wager, now we three are together again!"

"Aye. Bowgentle, have my armour brought. And where is my sword?"

"Count Brass—you must still be weak. . . ."

"Then bring me food—a great deal of food—and I'll fortify myself as we talk." And Count Brass sprang from his bed to embrace his daughter and her betrothed.

In the hall they ate while Dorian Hawkmoon told Count Brass all that had befallen him since leaving the castle so many months before. Count Brass, in turn, told of his tribulations with, it had seemed, the entire might of the Dark Empire to contend with. He told of von Villach's last battle and how the old man had died bravely, at the cost of a score of Dark Empire lives, how he, himself, had been wounded, how he had learned of Yisselda's disappearance and lost the will to live.

Oladahn came down then and was introduced. He said that D'Averc was badly hurt but that Bowgentle thought he would recover.

On the whole it was a cheerful homecoming, but marred by the knowledge that on the borders the Guardians were fighting for their lives, almost certainly fighting a losing battle.

Count Brass had by this time donned his armour of brass and strapped on his huge broadsword. He towered above the others as he stood up and said, "Come, Hawkmoon, Sir Oladahn, we must to the battlefield and lead our men to victory."

Bowgentle sighed. "Two hours ago I thought you all but dead—now you ride to battle. You are not well enough, sir."

"My sickness was of the spirit, not the flesh, and that's cured now," roared Count Brass. "Horses! Tell them to bring our horses, Sir Bowgentle!"

Though himself weary, Hawkmoon found renewed vigor as he followed the old man from the castle. He blew a kiss to Yisselda, and then they were in the courtyard, mounting the horses that would bear them to the battlefield.

They rode hard, the three of them, through the secret pathways of the marshlands, with huge clouds of giant flamingoes passing through the air over their heads, herds of wild horned horses galloping away from them. Count Brass waved a gloved hand. "Such a land is worth defending with all we have. Such peace is worth protecting."

Soon they heard the sounds of warfare and came to where the Dark Empire drove against the towers. They reined in when they saw the worst.

Count Brass spoke in a stricken whisper. "Impossible," he said.

But it was true.

The towers had fallen. Each lay broken, a pile of smoking masonry. The survivors were even now being pressed back, though they battled bravely.

"This is the fall of the Kamarg," said Count Brass in the voice of an old man.

Chapter Eleven

RETURN OF THE WARRIOR

Now ONE OF the captains saw them and came riding up. His armour was in tatters and his sword broken, but there was joy in his face. "Count Brass! At last! Come sir, we must rally the men—drive the Dark Empire dogs away!"

Hawkmoon saw Count Brass force himself to smile, draw his great broadsword, and say, "Aye, Captain. See if you can find a herald or two to tell all that Count Brass is back!"

A cheer went up from the hard-pressed Kamargians as Count Brass and Hawkmoon appeared, and they held their ground, even pushed the Granbretanians back in places. Count Brass, with Hawkmoon and Oladahn following, rode into the thick of his men, once again the invincible man of metal. "Aside, lads!" he called. "Aside and let me get at the enemy!"

Count Brass grabbed his own battered standard from a nearby rider, and with this balanced in the crook of his arm, his sword waving, he drove forward at the mass of beast masks ahead.

Hawkmoon rode up beside him, and they made a menacing, almost supernatural pair, the one in his flaming armor of brass and the other with the black jewel imbedded in his forehead, their swords rising and falling on the heads of the tightly packed Granbretan infantry. And when another figure joined them, a stocky man with fur covering his face and a flashing sabre striking here and there like lightning, they seemed a trio out of mythology, unnerving the beast warriors of Granbretan so that they fell back.

Hawkmoon searched about for Meliadus, swearing that he would certainly kill him this time, but he could not see him for the moment.

Gauntleted hands tried to drag him from his saddle, but his sword slipped through eyeholes, split helms, and sliced heads from their shoulders.

The day wore on, and the fighting continued without respite. Hawkmoon swayed in his saddle now, battle-weary and half-dazed with pain from a dozen minor cuts and a great many bruises. His horse was killed, but the weight of men surrounding him was so great that he sat it for half an hour before he realized it was dead. Then he sprang off it and continued fighting on foot.

He knew that no matter how many he and the others killed, they were outnumbered and ill-equipped. Gradually they were being driven farther and farther back.

"Ah," he murmured to himself, "if only we had a few hundred fresh troops, we might win the day. By the Runestaff, we need aid!"

Suddenly a strange electric sensation ran through his body, and he gasped, recognizing what was happening to him, realizing that he had unconsciously invoked the Runestaff. The Red Amulet, which now glowed at his neck, spreading red light on the armor of his enemies, was now transmitting power into his body. He laughed and began to hew around him with fantastic strength, cutting back the circle of warriors attacking him. His sword snapped, but he grabbed a lance from a horseman riding at him, dragged its owner from his saddle, and, swinging the lance like a sword, jumped onto the horse and resumed the attack.

"Hawkmoon! Hawkmoon!" he cried using the old battlecry of his ancestors. "Hai—Oladahn—Count Brass!" He gouged his way through the beast-masked warriors between himself and his friends. Count Brass's standard still swayed in its owner's hand.

"Drive them back!" Hawkmoon yelled. "Drive them back to our borders!"

Then Hawkmoon was everywhere, a whirling bringer of death. He raced through the ranks of Granbretan, and where he passed there were only corpses. A great muttering went up from the enemy then, and they began to falter.

Soon they were falling back, some actually running from the field. And then the figure of Baron Meliadus appeared, crying out to them to turn to stand and to fight.

"Back!" he cried. "You cannot fear so few!" But the tide was completely on the turn now, and he himself was caught by it, borne back by his retreating men.

They fled in terror from the pale-faced knight whose sword fell everywhere, in whose skull a black jewel shone and at whose throat hung an amulet of scarlet fire, whose fierce horse reared over their heads. They had heard, too, that he shouted the name of a dead man—that he, himself, was a dead man, Dorian Hawkmoon, who had fought against them at Köln and almost defeated them there, who had defied the King-Emperor himself, who had nearly slain Baron Meliadus and had, in fact, defeated him more than once. Hawkmoon! It was the only name the Dark Empire feared.

"Hawkmoon! Hawkmoon!" The figure held its sword high as its horse reared again. "Hawkmoon!"

Possessed of the power of the Red Amulet, Hawkmoon chased the fleeing army, and he laughed wildly with a mad triumph. Behind him rode Count Brass, terrible in his red-gold armour, his huge blade dripping with the blood of his foes; Oladahn, grinning through his fur, bright eyes gleaming, sabre slick with gore; and behind them the jubilant forces of the Kamarg, a handful of men jeering at the mighty army they had routed.

Now the power of the amulet began to fade from Hawkmoon, and he felt his pains return, felt the weariness again, but now it did not matter, for they had come to the border, marked by the ruined towers, and watched their enemies in flight.

Oladahn laughed. "Our victory, Hawkmoon."

Count Brass frowned. "Aye—but not one we can sustain. We must withdraw, regroup, find some safer ground to stand, for we will not beat them again in the open field."

"You are right," nodded Hawkmoon. "Now that the towers have fallen we need to find another spot well defended—and there is only one I can think of. . . ." He glanced at the Count.

"Aye—Castle Brass," agreed the old man. "We must send word to all the towns and villages of the Kamarg to tell the people to bring their goods and stock to Aigues-Mortes under the protection of the castle. . . ."

"Will we be able to sustain so many for a long siege?" Hawkmoon asked.

"We shall see," Count Brass replied, watching the distant army beginning to regroup. "But at least they will have some protection when the Dark Empire troops flood over our Kamarg."

There were tears in his eyes as he turned his horse and began to ride back to the castle.

From the balcony of his rooms in the eastern tower, Hawkmoon watched the people driving their livestock into the protection of the old town of Aigues-Mortes. Most of them were corralled in the amphitheater at one end of the town. Soldiers brought in provisions and helped folk with their loaded carts. By evening all but a few had entered the safety of the walls, crowding into houses or camping in the streets. Hawkmoon prayed that plague or panic might not set in, for such a crowd might be hard to control.

Oladahn joined him on the balcony, pointing to the northeast. "Look," he said. "Flying machines." And

Hawkmoon saw the ominous shapes of Dark Empire ornithopters flapping over the horizon, a certain sign that the army of Granbretan was on the move.

By nightfall, they could see the cooking fires of the nearest troops.

"Tomorrow," said Hawkmoon. "It could be our last battle."

They went down to the hall, where Bowgentle talked to Count Brass. Food had been prepared, as lavishly as ever. The two men turned as Hawkmoon and Oladahn entered the hall.

"How is D'Averc?" Hawkmoon asked.

"Stronger," Bowgentle said. "He has an excellent constitution, says he would like to get up to eat tonight. I said he might."

Yisselda came through the outer door. "I've spoken to the women," she said, "and they say all are within the walls. We have enough provisions to last as much as a year, if we slaughter the stock. . . ."

Count Brass smiled sadly. "It will take less than a year to decide this battle. And how is the spirit in the town?"

"Good," she said, "now that they have heard of your victory today and know you both to be alive."

"It is as well," Count Brass said heavily, "that they do not know that tomorrow they die. Or if not tomorrow, the next day. We cannot stand against such a weight of soldiers for long, my dear. Most of our flamingoes are dead, so we have virtually no protection in the air. Most of our Guardians are dead, and the troops we have left are all but untrained."

Bowgentle sighed. "And we thought the Kamarg could never fall. . . ."

"You are too certain that it will," said a voice from the stairs, and there was D'Averc, pale and dressed in a loose, fawn-colored gown, limping down to the hall. "In such spirits you are bound to lose. You could try to talk of victory, at least."

"You are right, Sir Huillam." Count Brass changed

his mood with an effort of will. "And we could eat some of this good food here to give us energy for tomorrow's struggle."

"How are you, D'Averc?" Hawkmoon asked as they seated themselves at the board.

"Well enough," said D'Averc lightly. "I think I can manage some small refreshments." And he began to heap his plate with meat.

They ate in silence, for the most part, relishing the meal that many felt would be their last.

When Hawkmoon looked from his window the next morning, it was to see the marshlands overlaid with men. In the night, the Dark Empire had crept up close to their walls, and now it was readying itself for the assault.

Quickly Hawkmoon donned clothes and armor and went down to the hall, where he found D'Averc already encased in his patched armor, Oladahn cleaning his blade, and Count Brass discussing some feature of the coming campaign with two of his remaining captains.

There was an atmosphere of tension in the hall, and the men spoke to one another in murmurs.

Yisselda appeared and called to him softly, "Dorian . . ." He turned and ran up the stairs to the landing on which she stood, taking her in his arms and holding her close, kissing her gently on the forehead. "Dorian," she said, "let us be married before . . ."

"Aye," he said quietly. "Let us find Bowgentle."

They found the philosopher in his quarters reading a book. He looked up as they entered and smiled at them. They told him what they wanted, and he laid down his book. "I had hoped for the grand ceremony," he said, "but I understand."

And he made them join hands and kneel before him while he spoke the words of his own composition that had always been used in marriages since he and his friend the Count had come to Castle Brass.

When it was done, Hawkmoon stood up and kissed Yisselda again. Then he said, "Look after her, Bowgentle," and left the room to join his friends, who were already leaving the hall for the courtyard.

As they mounted their horses a great shadow suddenly darkened the courtyard, and they heard the creaking and clattering overhead that could only be a Dark Empire ornithopter. A bolt of flame leapt from it and splashed on the cobbles, narrowly missing Hawkmoon and causing his horse to rear, nostrils flaring and eyes rolling.

Count Brass brought up the flame-lance with which he had already equipped himself and touched the stud, and red fire struck upwards at the flying machine. They heard the pilot scream and saw the thing's wings cease to work. It glided out of sight, and they heard it crash at last on the side of the hill.

"I must station flame-lancers in the towers," Count Brass said. "They'll have the best chance of striking back at the ornithopters. Come, gentlemen—let's to the battle."

And as they left the castle walls and rode down to the town, they saw the huge tide of men was already washing at the walls of the town where Kamarg warriors fought desperately to drive it back.

Ornithopters, fashioned like grotesque metal birds, wheeled over the town, pouring down flame into the streets, and the air became filled with the screams of the townsfolk, the roar of flame-lances, and the clash of metal against metal. Black smoke hung over Aigues-Mortes, and in places houses were already burning.

Hawkmoon led the charge down to the town and pushed through frightened women and children to gain the walls and join in the fight. Elsewhere were Count Brass, D'Averc, and Oladahn, helping to resist the force that tried to crush the town.

There came a desperate roar from one portion of the wall and an echoing cheer of triumph, and Hawkmoon began to run in that direction, seeing that a hole had been breached in the defenses and Dark Empire warriors, in helms of wolf and bear, were gushing through.

Hawkmoon met them, and they wavered instantly, remembering his earlier exploits. He was no longer equipped with superhuman strength, but he used the pause to cry his ancestral battleshout, "Hawkmoon! Hawkmoon!" and leap at them, sword meeting metal, flesh, and bone and driving them back through the breach.

So they fought all day, holding the town even as their numbers rapidly dropped, and when the night fell and the Dark Empire troops withdrew, Hawkmoon knew, as they all knew, that the next morning must bring defeat.

Wearily, Hawkmoon, Count Brass, and the others led their horses back up the winding road to the castle, their hearts heavy as they thought of all the innocents slaughtered that day and of all the innocents who would be slaughtered tomorrow—if they were lucky enough to die.

Then they heard a galloping horse behind them and turned on the slope, swords ready, to see the strange figure of a tall rider coming up the hill toward the castle. He had a long helm that completely encased his face, and his armor was wrought all in jet and gold. Hawkmoon scowled. "What does that traitorous thief want?" he said.

The Warrior in Jet and Gold pulled up his big horse nearby. His deep, vibrant voice came from within his helmet then. "Greetings, defenders of the Kamarg. I see the day goes badly for you. Baron Meliadus will defeat you tomorrow."

Hawkmoon wiped his forehead with a rag. "No need to make so much of the obvious, Warrior. What have you come to steal this time?"

"Nothing," said the warrior. "I have come to deliver something." He reached behind him and produced Hawkmoon's battered saddlebags.

Hawkmoon's spirits rose, and he leaned forward to take the saddlebags, opening one to look inside. There, wrapped in a cloak, was the object he had been given so long ago by Rinal. It was safe. He pulled back the cloak and saw the crystal unshattered.

"But why did you take it in the first place?" he asked.

"Let us go to Castle Brass, and there I will explain all to you," said the warrior.

In the hall the warrior stood up by the fireplace while the others sat in various positions around him, listening.

"At the Mad God's castle," began the warrior, "I left you because I knew that with the aid of the Mad God's beasts you could soon be safely away from there. But I knew other hazards lay ahead of you and suspected that you might be captured. Therefore, I decided to take the object Rinal gave you and keep it safe until you should return to the Kamarg."

"And I had thought you a thief!" Hawkmoon said. "I am sorry, Warrior."

"But what is the object?" Count Brass asked.

"An ancient machine," the Warrior said, "produced by one of the most sophisticated sciences ever to emerge on this earth."

"A weapon?" Count Brass asked.

"No. It is a device which can warp whole areas of time and space and shift them into other dimensions. While the machine exists, it can exert this power, but should it, by mischance, be destroyed, then the area it has warped falls immediately back into the time and space original to it."

"And how is it operated?" Hawkmoon asked, remembering suddenly that he had no such knowledge.

"It is difficult to explain, since you would recognize none of the words I would use," said the Warrior in Jet and Gold. "But Rinal has taught me its use, among other things, and I can work it."

"But for what purpose?" D'Averc asked. "To shift the troublesome Baron and his men to some limbo where they will not bother us again?"

"No," said the Warrior. "I will explain—"

The doors burst open, and a battered soldier rushed into the hall. "Master," he cried to Count Brass, "it is Baron Meliadus under a flag of truce. He would parley with you at the town walls."

"I have nothing to say to him," Count Brass said.

"He says that he intends to attack at night. That he can have the walls down within an hour, for he has fresh troops held back for the purpose. He says that if you deliver your daughter, Hawkmoon, D'Averc, and yourself into his hands, he will be lenient with the rest."

Count Brass thought for a moment, but Hawkmoon broke in, "It is useless to consider such a bargain, Count Brass. We both know of Meliadus's penchant for treachery. He seeks only to demoralize the folk to make his victory easier."

Count Brass sighed. "But if what he says is true, and I cannot doubt that it is, he will have the walls down shortly and we all perish."

"With honour, at least," said D'Averc.

"Aye," said Count Brass with a somewhat sardonic smile. "With honour, at least." He turned to the courier. "Tell Baron Meliadus that we still do not wish to speak with him."

The warrior bowed. "I will, my lord." He left the hall.

"We had best return to the walls," said Count Brass, rising wearily just as Yisselda entered the room.

"Ah, Father, Dorian—you are both safe."

Hawkmoon embraced her. "But now we must go back," he said softly. "Meliadus is about to launch another attack."

"Wait," said the Warrior in Jet and Gold. "I have yet to describe my plan to you."

Chapter Twelve
ESCAPE TO LIMBO

BARON MELIADUS SMILED when he heard the courier's message.

"Very well," he said to his stewards, "let the whole town be destroyed and as many of its inhabitants taken alive to give us sport on our victory day." He turned his horse back to where his fresh troops awaited him.

"Move forward," he said, and watched as they began to flow towards the doomed town and the castle beyond.

He saw the fires on the town walls, the few soldiers waiting, knowing with certainty that they would die. He saw the graceful outlines of the castle that had once protected the town so well, and he chuckled. There was a warmth inside him, for he had longed for this victory ever since he had been ejected from the castle some two years earlier.

Now his troops had nearly reached the walls, and he kicked his horse's flanks to make it move down so that he could see the battle better.

Then he frowned. There seemed something wrong with the light, for the outline of town and castle had apparently wavered in a most alarming fashion.

He opened his mask and rubbed at his eyes, then looked again.

The silhouette of Castle Brass and Aigues-Mortes seemed to glow, first pink, then pale red, then scarlet, and Baron Meliadus felt lightheaded. He licked his dry lips and feared for his sanity.

The troops had paused in their attack, muttering to themselves and backing away from the place. The entire town and the hillside and castle it surrounded were now a flaming blue. The blue began to fade, and fading with it went Castle Brass and Aigues-Mortes. A wild wind blew, knocking Baron Meliadus back in his saddle.

He cried out, "Guards! What has happened?"

"The place has—has vanished, my lord," came a nervous voice.

"Vanished! Impossible. How can a whole town and a hill vanish? It is still there. They have erected some kind of screen around the place."

Baron Meliadus rode wildly down to where the town walls had been, expecting to meet a barrier, but none blocked him, and his horse trampled over only mud that looked as if it had been recently ploughed.

"They have escaped me!" he howled. "But how? What science aids them? What power can they have that is greater than mine?"

The troops had begun to turn back. Some were running. But Baron Meliadus dismounted from his horse, hands outstretched, trying to feel for the vanished town. He screamed with fury and wept with impotent rage, falling at last to his knees in the mud and shaking his fist at where Castle Brass had been.

"I will find you, Hawkmoon—and your friends. I will bring all the scientific knowledge of Granbretan to bear on this search. And I will follow you, if needs be, to whatever place you have escaped to, whether it be on this earth or beyond it, and you will know my vengeance. By the Runestaff, I swear this!"

And then he looked up as he heard the thump of a horse's hooves riding past him, thought he saw a figure flash by in armour of jet and gold, thought he heard ghostly ironic laughter, and then the rider, too, had vanished.

Baron Meliadus rose up from his knees and looked around him for his horse.

"Oh, Hawkmoon," he said through clenched teeth. "Oh, Hawkmoon, I will catch thee!"

Again he had sworn by the Runestaff, as on that fateful morning two years before. And his action had set in motion a new pattern of history. His second oath strengthened that pattern, whether it favoured Meliadus or Hawkmoon, and hardened all their destinies a little more strongly.

Baron Meliadus found his horse and returned to his camp. Tomorrow he would leave for Granbretan and the labyrinth laboratories of the Order of the Snake. Sooner or later he would be bound to find a way through to the vanished Castle Brass, he told himself.

Yisselda looked through the window in wonderment, her face alight with joy. Hawkmoon smiled down at her and hugged her to him.

Behind them, Count Brass coughed and said, "To tell you the truth, my children, I'm a little disturbed by all this—this *science*. Where did that fellow say we were?"

"In some other Kamarg, father," said Yisselda.

The view from the window was misty. Though the town and the hillside were solid enough, the rest was not. Beyond it they could see, as if through a blue radiance, shining lagoons and waving reeds, but they were of transformed colours, no longer of simple greens and yellows, but of all the colours of the rainbow and without the substance of the castle and its surrounds.

"He said we might explore it," said Hawkmoon. "So it must be more tangible than it looks."

D'Averc cleared his throat. "I'll stay here and in the town, I think. What say you, Oladahn?"

Oladahn grinned. "I think so—until I'm more used to it, at least."

"Well, I'm with you," said Count Brass. He laughed. "Still, we're safe, eh? And our people, too. We've that to be grateful for."

"Aye," said Bowgentle thoughtfully. "But we must not underestimate the scientific prowess of Granbretan. If there is a way of following us here, they will find it —be sure of that."

Hawkmoon nodded. "You are right, Bowgentle." He

pointed to Rinal's gift, which lay now in the center of the empty dining table, outlined in the strange, pale blue light that flooded through the windows. "We must keep that in our safest vault. Remember what the warrior said—if it is destroyed, we find ourselves back again in our own space and time."

Bowgentle went over to the machine and gently picked it up. "I will see that it is safe," he said.

When he had left, Hawkmoon turned again to look through the window, fingering the Red Amulet.

"The Warrior said that he would come again with a message and a mission for me," he said. "I am in no doubt now that I serve the Runestaff, and when the Warrior comes, I shall have to leave Castle Brass, leave this sanctuary, and return again to the world. You must be prepared for that, Yisselda."

"Let us not speak of it now," she said, "but celebrate, instead, our marriage."

"Aye, let us do that," he said with a smile. But he could not shut entirely from his mind the knowledge that somewhere, separated from him by subtle barriers, the world still existed and was still in danger from the Dark Empire. Though he appreciated the respite, the time to spend with the woman he loved, he knew that soon he must return to that world and do battle once more with the forces of Granbretan.

But for the moment, he would be happy.

(This ends the Second Volume of the High
History of the Runestaff)